Love & Blessings!!
Joanne

THE SOROTI PROJECT

A Heart-Filled and Heartless Story in Uganda

JOANNE NORTON

D1521987

Editing and design by Fistbump Media, LLC

ISBN: 1514307332
ISBN-13: 978-1514307335

APPRECIATION

This story is primarily from my time in Soroti. I ministered at a couple other places with:

Tim and Jill Way, who now live in Tulsa, OK, but have lived in Uganda much of the time for the last twenty years, who used me in Kabujogera in the southwest portion of the country. I taught spiritual mapping and spiritual warfare for local and not-so-local pastors who came on bicycles or the back of trucks for the conference. Most of the pastors had very little income, and had only to pay the equivalent of about two dollars for Tim's ministry teaching book. The few days there were amazing, and they also hosted me for a few days in Masaka. They have been wonderful to us over the years we have known them.

The very special people of New Hope Uganda, an excellent orphanage Jay and Vickie Dangers began in 1986. When I wasn't in Soroti, I stayed at New Hope some of the time. My husband Dave and I had ministered there in the nineties, and we had some wonderful times.

Thanks to those who have encouraged me, offered suggestions, and edited the book:

- David Norton, my husband
- Susan Jones, my long-time friend
- Kay Osika, my Christian counselor and friend
- Blog friends and readers, far too many to list.

CONTENTS

INTRODUCTION AND INFORMATION.................1

PROLOGUE...3
CHAPTER ONE...3
CHAPTER TWO..15
CHAPTER THREE....................................23
CHAPTER FOUR......................................29
CHAPTER FIVE..35
CHAPTER SIX...39
CHAPTER SEVEN 45
CHAPTER EIGHT.....................................47
CHAPTER NINE 51
CHAPTER TEN...55
CHAPTER ELEVEN 63
CHAPTER TWELVE..................................67
CHAPTER THIRTEEN 83
CHAPTER FOURTEEN...........................85
CHAPTER FIFTEEN 91
CHAPTER SIXTEEN.................................95
CHAPTER SEVENTEEN 101
CHAPTER EIGHTEEN 105
CHAPTER NINETEEN............................109
CHAPTER TWENTY................................113
CHAPTER TWENTY-ONE.......................115
CHAPTER TWENTY-TWO 121
CHAPTER TWENTY-THREE 123
CHAPTER TWENTY-FOUR 127
CHAPTER TWENTY-FIVE 131
CHAPTER TWENTY-SIX.........................135
CHAPTER TWENTY-SEVEN...................143
CHAPTER TWENTY-EIGHT 147
CHAPTER TWENTY-NINE......................151
CHAPTER THIRTY...................................155
CHAPTER THIRTY-ONE 161
CHAPTER THIRTY-TWO.........................167
CHAPTER THIRTY-THREE 175
CHAPTER THIRTY-FOUR........................179

CHAPTER THIRTY-FIVE 183
CHAPTER THIRTY-SIX 189
EPILOGUE 195

DEDICATION AND EXPLANATION 197

INTRODUCTION AND INFORMATION

About eleven years ago, I was called to minister in Uganda, primarily in Soroti, in the north. While I also spent time in Kampala and other locations, Soroti was the most important during that time. While I was there I sent many emails to my husband, friends and church members, and when I returned, they were very encouraging about the work I had done.

I started this book several years ago. I later started and finished the book *The Annie Project*, and part of that book has one of the main characters (me) visiting Soroti. I then adjusted this book to fit the *The Annie Project*. While both books are fictional, parts of *Annie* and much of this book are largely factual, particularly the emails. The parts of this book set in Kampala and Jinja are a bit more fictionalized than the part set in Soroti.

As in my first book, I go by "Cary". My given name is Carolyn Joanne; I have always gone by my middle name, but I use "Cary" for my stories.

The time in Soroti was very special, very important, and very heart-opening. I was protected several times from danger. At the Omaha airport before I left, my husband and I were concerned that I might not be coming back. Our love was intense, but we knew God had called me to go and we needed to obey. It truly was a miracle that I was protected and healed.

Thank you and bless you for reading.

PROLOGUE

Cary had been in London's Heathrow Airport for twelve hours. She wanted to call home to Newton and decided to call Pastor Max instead of her kids—he would want to know more details and would spread the news better. She punched the numbers; the phone rang a few times, and she breathed a sigh of relief when he answered.

"Hi, Pastor Max. I'm in London, and I've explored a little bit, but it gets dark so early here in the winter, so now I'm only wandering around Heathrow. The time difference is a challenge, to say the least."

"Oh, it's good to hear from you, Cary. I can't remember the timing, though."

"Well, it's six hours later here, so when it's ten o'clock in the morning London time, it's four o'clock in the morning for you—and for my body. It's hard for me to adjust, but going downtown on a subway train and then getting on the top of the buses to see London is fun, so I manage to stay awake."

"Did you meet anyone or see anything interesting? And how's the food?"

Cary laughed. "I met a lady who is going to Uganda to be with her daughter who has been there for a couple years and has some orphan kids living with her in Jinja. The lady, Linda, wants to meet her new Ugandan grandkids. We met at the bathroom at the airport this morning while I was brushing my teeth, and we went to town together. We went to the famous Harrods for lunch. The cost was horrific. A normal-sized soup, salad, and pop came to thirty dollars. I was shocked!"

"When do you leave for Uganda? And when will you get there?"

"I'll be leaving about eleven o'clock tonight and get there between nine and ten in the morning. Since its three hours later than here, my body will be struggling again."

"When will you be calling FAITH and connecting with them?"

"Well, I'll be staying with my Ugandan son, Sam. He'll call FAITH, and he can probably take me to Soroti in about a week. I'll connect with FAITH people there or nearby. I'll do my God-job, whatever it takes."

Pastor Max laughed. "Yes, Cary, I know you'll do whatever you can whenever you can to serve our Lord."

Cary laughed, too. "You've made me smile. I'm very tired and might doze a bit on the plane tonight, which isn't normal. But I don't have my husband with me, of course, so it's a *lot* different to be heading to Uganda."

"Well, your name will be spread around the church and the town and you will be prayed for, over and over again."

"Thank you *so much*. I appreciate you and my family and friends. I'd better go now—it's expensive to talk."

"I understand. Keep in touch, though. And I'll call Sue, Mike, and Luke right away."

Suddenly Cary said, "Oh, one more thing you can spread around. Last night on the plane when I was standing by the toilets, I had a conversation with a lady named Rahajina. Her parents were from India, but she had been born in the States and had been living in D.C. and London since she had married. Her husband was originally from India and they now had two small children. Her husband had decided to return to India. She was very upset, because his mom had already said to him that she hates Rahajina, because Rahajina was *not* the girl she had chosen for him to marry. Rahajina teared up when she talked about leaving all her family and friends behind and how hard the road ahead looked. I told her my church

4

people would pray and be standing with her. I prayed for her that God's grace would be with her and our Lord would meet her. I'm guessing she's Hindu by what I saw on her jewelry and her face. Anyhow, last night was truly an amazing 'divine appointment'. So please add her to the prayer list."

Pastor Max said, "Will do, Cary. God is obviously using you before you get to your target."

Cary laughed. "Yes, one of my main personal quotes is 'being in the right place at the right time'. Thank you. Now, I *will* say goodbye."

And she did.

They each hung up laughing and rejoicing.

JOANNE NORTON

CHAPTER ONE

"This is your captain speaking. In twenty minutes we will be landing in Entebbe. Shortly, the flight attendants will be going through the cabin to pick up any items you wish to discard. Please continue to obey the safety signs. Thank you for flying with British Airways."

The captain's voice woke Cary, startling her out of a fairly deep sleep. Sunlight hit her squarely in the eyes as it burst through the window next to the seat in front of her, her own window still being shaded. Cary scrambled to get a flight attendant's attention, as she didn't have the landing card needed to get through customs. She wondered whether or not her luggage had made the flight with her; she knew it had been left behind in Chicago, but wasn't sure whether it had somehow caught up with her during the fourteen hour layover in London.

As soon as the attendant approached her, Cary asked, "Did my bags make it?"

"Sorry, but no," the attendant said as she handed Cary the landing card. "I came to tell you during the night, but you were always asleep. You slept better than any passenger on the flight."

Cary shook her head in amazement. Not about the luggage; she had expected that. But it was a minor miracle that she had slept so much. She remembered waking a bit when dinner was passed around, the aroma intruding into her exhaustion, but she had been too tired to eat. Later, she woke up quite chilled, so she scrounged through the overhead bin to find a sweater. Other than grabbing the pillow, shifting stiff limbs and adjusting her pillow, she had slept nearly eight hours from the time the plane was taxiing to the runway at Heathrow until this point near touchdown in Uganda.

Cary had taken this London-to-Entebbe flight a number of times over the years, but this was definitely the first time she had slept well. Ever since her first flight in her early twenties, her family and friends had called her a "white knuckle flyer", so this sleep was especially appreciated.

As the plane began its descent, the adrenalin started pumping and Cary pressed her face as close to the window as possible. Her eyes widened and her heart swelled as she looked at the sapphire blue of Lake Victoria with its many islands, the palm trees meeting the shoreline, red ribbons of road stretching off into the hills around the airport, and the small houses tucked under the canopies of the trees with their gardens spread around them. One of Cary's favorite sights when she lived in Uganda was the flocks of egrets, and she was overjoyed as she saw some of the beautiful white birds flying among the trees. When the plane landed and its door opened, the first thing she noticed was the smells: the sweet, musky scent of burning wood and masses of vegetation, and even a little garbage odor. She grinned. She felt right at home.

After a round of paperwork to get the search started for her luggage, Cary hurried through customs and out to see her family. Cary and her husband had gained a Ugandan son a few years earlier during a missionary stint; they had last been over for his wedding four years earlier. Now she was to meet her dear ones and their little two-and-a-half year old, Stella.

When Cary entered the reception area it took a few seconds for her eyes to adjust to the shadows and to find her family in the crowd. Then, suddenly, they stepped forward. Cary rushed over and threw her arms around them.

"Oh, it's so good to see you. I've missed you so much," exclaimed Cary. "You look *wonderful*!" Sam and Adhe wore beautiful cultural Ugandan clothing, all golds and greens with embroidery at the neckline and, in Adhe's case, the bottom of her dress, and in his, the bottom of his shirt.

Cary knelt before Stella, who said, "Hello, Grand-Ma," very carefully articulated, and stood very patiently and serenely as Cary administered her first hug.

Cary smiled up at Sam and Adhe. "You did really well! She's a sweetheart." And Cary stood and said, "And I need to hug you two from your dad who is in heaven, and he would *love* to be with you. But heaven is most important, doncha think?" And she winked at them.

Adhe pulled her arm from behind her back, and, with a sweet smile, gave Cary a huge bouquet of flowers. Cary was flooded with joy as she saw roses, frangipani, mini-carnations, gardenias, and beautiful fern-like greenery. It was a beautiful mass of color, and the scent was heavenly.

Cary stood back and shook her head. "Not only do your flowers look wonderful, but so do you in your glorious clothes. And here I am in wrinkled jeans and this baggy shirt. I look like a peasant and you look like royalty. I'd like to fix that, but with my luggage missing, I can't pop into the ladies' room and change. In fact, I have no idea what I'm going to do."

Adhe laughed. "We are just happy you are here, Mum[1]. We're so glad you've come and we don't care what you are wearing. I'm certain God will help with this challenge."

Although she joked about it, Cary was seriously concerned about the way she was dressed. Jeans would not be much of a problem in Kampala, being relatively modern, with quite a few people from Europe and North America. Sam and Adhe lived out in the "bush"—a rural area, where custom required that ladies wear dresses or skirts. Cary needed to replace her jeans as soon as possible.

With Sam carrying her carry-on bag and backpack, and Adhe holding Stella by one hand and Cary by the other, they made their way out to the car.

"I'm glad you were a few minutes late," Adhe said. "The security at the entrance to the airport was very strict today. Something must have happened. We were in line for quite some time. I was worried that you would be here and think we were somehow not coming."

"I guess losing the luggage was beneficial then." Cary said. "The plane was a few minutes early, but it took me nearly half an hour to get the paperwork finished. *I* was worried about *you* waiting here and thinking that maybe I had missed the flight out of London."

They laughed about all the "worrying" they had done when God, as usual, had everything under control.

Immediately, the issue of British cars and rules of the road confused Cary. She went to the wrong side of the car to be let in. "Oops! It's going to take me a while to get that through my head again. And once we hit the road, I'll be in even worse shape, constantly ducking because I think someone is coming at us on the wrong side of the road. It's always hard on my stomach and heart until my brain gets readjusted." They laughed together.

They headed to Kampala, Uganda's capital, about thirty miles north of Entebbe. Compared to her first trip into Uganda fifteen years earlier, the road was now well maintained. However, a zillion more cars were on the highway. What had *not* changed was the drivers' need to dodge motorcycles that zig-zagged dangerously in and out of traffic loaded with people, shop goods, bicycles, pedestrians, cattle, goats, and chickens. Cary closed her eyes in fear more than once and gripped the hand strap over her door, certain of a collision. Thankfully, it never happened.

As Sam was the owner and administrative manager of his project named Sanyu[2] Home, he had a long list of errands to run in the city. Cary was surprised at the increase in traffic in the four years since she'd visited. "How does anyone get around?" Cary asked. "It's one big traffic jam."

Sam laughed. "I refuse to look at the guy who wants to push in, and I slowly go through." Having said this, he slid into a space in the traffic, practically brushing the fender of another car as he pulled forward. Cary was sure he was going to lose his side mirror in the attempt. She cringed, waiting for the sound of metal scraping metal. Adhe, looking very cool and confident in her husband's driving, laughed quietly and patted Cary's shoulder. Within a few minutes, Sam had not only maneuvered his way into the busiest part of downtown without damaging either the car or the passengers, but, miracle of miracles, had found a parking space. He let Adhe and Cary out—unheard of for a Ugandan man—then took off one direction, up the hill to the main post office and the banking district. Cary, Adhe and Stella went down the hill, slithering around cars trapped at a traffic roundabout, and took off into the jam-packed middle of the Nakasero marketplace for their own shopping expedition.

Cary quickly found her old walking routine falling into place. She always watched where she was stepping in case a manhole cover or a whole slab of sidewalk was missing. She had recently heard the sad story of a bicycle rider who had not seen a missing cover during a rainstorm and had been swept into the hole, bicycle and all, and drowned. She quickly shifted her backpack so it hung across her chest. That way, she could hold it close to her body with her arm and no one could approach it without her noticing. Thievery was a huge problem. On previous visits, she had had a watch ripped off her wrist, and had seen the manhole covers stolen and houses completely stripped of all electrical and plumbing lines and equipment. In spite of the suddenness of the cultural shift, and her tiredness, Cary's senses were on alert. Newton was a world away, in more ways than just the ten thousand miles.

Cary hurried along beside Adhe. Adhe grabbed her hand and said, "Come in here, Mum," and ducked down a dark passageway between two buildings. It took a few seconds for Cary's eyes to adjust to the dimness. As soon as they were beyond the building walls, Cary found they were in an area of many small shops.

"How long have these shops been here?" Cary asked. "I don't remember ever seeing them."

"Many years. It's just that most 'muzungu'[3] never find out about it." Adhe grinned. "This is where the Ugandans buy their clothes."

After passing several shops, Adhe stopped. "This belongs to a cousin." She quietly spoke to the young woman sitting in front of the door. The usual formal, quiet, and lengthy greetings took place. The greetings consisted of inquiries about the day, the home family, and other relatives. This was not just because Adhe was a relative but because it is how Ugandans greet each other. Cary stood back patiently and waited. She had learned a few of the phrases over the years. The only word she recognized was "nyabo"[4]; it took a few moments for her to realize the word was being spoken to her. She had begun to zone out in the heat and the drone of the voices.

A shop girl asked, "Nyabo, would you like to sit?" and pointed to a small wooden stool next to the counter. Cary gratefully dropped onto the stool and put the backpack on the ground between her feet.

Adhe smiled at Cary. "You look very tired, so I will shop and return for you. My cousin, Margaret, will take care of anything you need. Be free."

Adhe took Stella's hand and they ducked down another passage Cary had not noticed. For a while, Cary looked around taking in her surroundings. Most shops were only six feet wide and less than ten feet deep. Bare light bulbs hung from electric cords, but as there was no power at the moment, the only light was whatever sunlight managed to filter down from between the buildings surrounding the alley. Electricity was obviously as frustratingly unreliable as Cary remembered it to be.

Cary sat and watched the people milling around. She listened to their speech—some spoke English with a distinct British accent, while some spoke Luganda or another tribal language. She suddenly felt very much at home. She was always astounded how much more comfortable she was in the Ugandan or African atmosphere than she was in middle-America. She was never certain why that was so, but she knew God had placed a love for these people in her heart.

She felt a hand on her shoulder. "Mum," Adhe was saying. "It's time to leave."

Cary hadn't realized she had fallen asleep. As she jerked to attention she grabbed for her backpack. She let out a big sigh of relief. "It's still here."

The shop girl said, "Of course, Madam; no one would take it. I have been here all this time, watching."

"Of course; I'm sorry. Thank you so much. And thank you for letting me sit for so long. I didn't realize how tired I had become."

Adhe said, "Sam is waiting for us. I found most things we needed and he finished his work more quickly than he thought, so we may reach home earlier than we planned."

They worked their way out of town through a maze of side streets. Cary sat back and looked at all the neighborhoods and buildings she recognized from her months of living in Kampala. It was as if no time had passed. They turned on to Makerere Road, near the university, and Cary said, "Oh! My old stomping grounds. I know Sam knows all this, but we didn't have much time surrounding your wedding to tell you all the stories, Adhe. At one time, I knew this area better than any in town. We went to the Baptist church, the Full Gospel church, shopped in the Nakulabye and Wandageya market places, and lived in the slums for a month." Cary laughed. "*That* was an experience—for our hosts, the Mugarukas, and their neighbors, as well as for us. One lady on the path to the back side of Nakulabye used us to scare her little girl. When we showed up, I'm sure she said we were something like what we'd call a 'boogie man' and the poor child would scream and hide her face in her mother's skirt. In downtown Kampala, white faces were pretty common; back there, a white person was rarely seen along their paths, especially by little children."

At the next major intersection, Cary was surprised again. "A traffic light? A *real* traffic light? Since when?"

Sam answered, "They redid this intersection about a year ago. There were too many accidents. So, they tried to make it safer by adding the light." He glanced at Cary with a bit of a grin. "Actually, the city has put in *two* traffic lights since you were last here; this one, and one on the other side of town. That makes five all together."

Cary laughed. "Aren't they afraid they'll become too safety conscious? After all, the couple million people living here are used to dodging through traffic. Traffic lights might make them lose their survival skills." They all laughed.

In a few minutes, they had picked their way through town and headed out towards the north, on Bombo Road, through Bwaise, Kawempe, and Matuuga. The exhaust fumes, heat, dust, and general odors had a wearing effect on Cary. After Matuuga, once they were past the seemingly never-ending traffic congestion and the swarms of people, bicycles, longhorn cattle, dogs, and goats, Cary settled back and looked across the fields. The rolling hills were dotted with banana and palm trees waving in the breeze, and the clouds piled on top of each other all the way to the horizon.

"I can't believe this," she said to Adhe and Sam. "I slept on the plane, and fell asleep in the shop, and now I'm having trouble keeping my eyes open. But I don't want to miss *anything*."

For a few minutes, they buzzed along the highway with little to get in their way, Cary and Adhe catching up on all the news from family and friends. Suddenly Sam hit a huge pothole, and the car jerked towards the road edge. Cary and Adhe cried out in shock and surprise.

"Sorry," Sam said. "I forgot about that one and didn't see it until too late."

Soon after, Sam turned off the main road and went down an unpaved side road, cluttered with potholes.

"What's going on?" Cary asked.

"You'll see," Adhe said with a mischievous smile. "You have some friends who recently moved and we are going to see them." Sam slowed to a crawl and bumped his way along. Then he turned down an even *less* maintained path. Cary took in the gardens and small homes. Most had metal roofs, but some were fitted with traditional thatch.

Adhe said, with that same smile, "I told you earlier that God would help us with the challenge of finding you some clothes. I believe He has."

They pulled up under a mango tree next to a concrete-over-baked-brick-style home. It could have blended in anywhere, except for the water tower attached to the back of the house and the abundance of solar panels.

After a few seconds, their friend Alison came through the front door. "Sam, Adhe, what are you doing here? Come in, come in." Then she stopped and stared. "*Cary*? My goodness, it's wonderful to see you. I'd heard you were coming, but forgot how soon." While she spoke she hugged Cary and herded all of them into the living room. "Richard and the kids will be so disappointed to have missed you. Let me get you some juice. I'm sure you could use a cold drink."

Cary was blessed to hear Alison's strong British accent. It brought back so many memories of time spent with Alison and Richard and their children.

After all the greetings and getting caught up on the recent news, Adhe finally said, "We have a problem and we hope you can help. Mum's luggage didn't come and this is all she has to wear."

Alison jumped up out of her chair. "Most certainly I can help. Come to my room."

Cary sat on the bed while Alison went through her clothes, holding up one after the other. "I think this blue dress should work for you, and this will be good enough for church, and here's a skirt and blouse and a nightdress." All the while she was talking, she was pulling more clothes out from under the bed, and off of dresser tops. She laughed and said, "I've never become used to living without clothes cupboards. I won't need any of this for a while, so you just don't worry about it. Bring them back when you can." She looked down. "You'll need some sandals, too. You can't wear those heavy shoes around." She got down on her hands and knees and dug around in a box at the foot of her bed, first taking a quick look through for cockroaches, ants, and spiders. "I think these sandals should do. They might be a bit big, but the straps tighten pretty well."

Cary said, "Alison, I can't thank you enough. You've made life so much easier for me. I really was worried about how I was going to make it until my bags came."

"I remember the times you left clothes behind when you visited and the times you sent gifts across with people who were coming here. You and James supplied plenty for me and many others over the years. I'm happy to have a chance to return the blessing."

After a few more minutes of visiting, Sam said, "Sorry, but if we are to reach home before dark, we must go." He turned to Alison. "I'll try to get Mom back here for lunch some time. I also need to talk to Richard for advice about what trees to plant on our new land. I'll try to call ahead to make sure he is here."

Cary shook her head. "Calling ahead. What a concept. *That* sure wasn't possible a few years ago. When *we* lived here only the richest and nearest to Kampala had a chance to have *home* phones."

As they were climbing into the car, Alison said, "Nearly everyone has a phone now. It's good, but it's also annoying. Ugandans have always had a polite society. Now, if a phone rings, people will answer and talk right in a meeting without even excusing themselves. It's as if they simply don't have any rules in place for this new invention, so they don't put any restrictions. I'm sure you'll face this sooner or later. Just as in England and the States, it has caused tragedies. The wife of a wealthy Indian businessman in Kampala died just a few weeks ago when she was talking on her mobile. She drove onto railroad tracks and was killed by a train. She didn't hear it coming. It's so sad." She paused and hugged Cary. "I look forward to visiting again. As Sam said, he will bring you for lunch one day."

Cary returned Alison's hug. "Thanks again for the clothes. Now I can relax a bit."

From that point on, from Alison's house, through Bombo and Wobulenzi, Cary had no more difficulty staying awake. She was excited to have clothes to wear, and talking about the various pieces of news Alison had shared kept Cary and Adhe yakking away.

They turned off of the main road near the market town of Luweero.

"Wow!" exclaimed Cary. "The roads! It actually looks like they've been grading and paving this section."

Sam nodded. "They have been working on it for a few months. Of course, when the rainy season starts, they lose time and some of the road washes away, but they hope to be through our general area in a few months."

"I remember the first time James and I were here in January of '91. The road was so bad it took forty minutes to travel just eleven miles. It was nearly all pot hole with one narrow ribbon of road, the undercarriage of the car was scraped many times, and when the road passed through the papyrus swamp the bridge was in very bad condition. Most of the way, the elephant grass was about eight feet high right up to the edge of the road and we saw hardly anyone along the route, no houses, nothing like it is today. I actually got a little frightened and thought, 'These people who are driving us out here could kill us and no one would ever find the bodies.'"

Adhe and Sam nodded at this. They understood that fear. Although young at the time, they had lived through Uganda's civil wars, and both had lost family members, killed either during the fighting or by being abducted and murdered by one faction or another. It was a very dangerous time for everyone, whether they lived in big cities, small towns, villages, or the bush. Even though they remembered the days of fear, they knew that by the time Cary had visited Uganda the first time, that sort of evil was behind them.

Cary sat back and smiled. She and James had been blessed, because Sam and Adhe survived and grew up into godly young people and had become their children, their dear ones. Cary and James couldn't have been more grateful.

----

1 "Mum" is British for "mother". Uganda had been a British Protectorate, so they spoke British English. Sam, having had a lot of contact with American missionaries, and having lived in the United States with Cary and James for a time, used the American term, "Mom".

2 "Joy".

3 "Muzungu" means "White person".

4 Nyabo is Ugandan for "Madam".

CHAPTER TWO

Right after they passed through the small town of Kiwoko[1], the car headed up the hill towards Sam and Adhe's property. Cary leaned forward, anxious to see every detail of their new home. "I can hardly stand it. I'm sure the photos you've sent won't do anything justice."

Sam laughed quietly. "It was a lot of work to build, but we are pleased. Willie was our contractor, and he chose good men for the job. The amazing part was that both the men and building supplies were here when needed."

Cary laughed, knowing that so often the opposite occurred. "You're right, Sam. That *is* a miracle."

Suddenly, as they came around a curve in the road, the house was nearly in front of them. Like other Ugandans, Sam's property had more than just one structure. Besides the main house, Cary saw a cookhouse, a storehouse, a latrine, and, set back from the main house, a building she assumed was for guests. The flowers surrounding both houses were beautiful and the bougainvillea bushes were wreathed in orange, white and magenta. Even during this dry season, with fewer flowers growing in the heat and lack of moisture, the multicolored zinnias, the bright yellow shrimp flowers, and vibrant red cannas made Cary grin. "I have missed color so much. This time of year at home, *everything* is brown and gray."

When the car stopped, two teenaged girls came out to greet them. Cary immediately recognized one of the girls. "Mary! What are you doing here?"

Mary ran to Cary and hugged her, and took the backpack out of her hand. "I have a break from school, so I decided to come and help Uncle Sam and Aunt Adhe. And, of course, I had heard you were coming, and I wanted to be here to welcome you."

Cary squeezed Mary's shoulders. "I'm glad you came. It is good to see you. And you have grown into a beautiful young lady."

"Thank you, Grandma[2]."

Adhe said, "Before we go into our house, I need to show you where you will be staying."

Mary carried the backpack. Cary hooked the plastic bag of clothes over her arm so she could hold Stella's hand. It was a very short walk to the guest house.

When they opened the door, Cary was immediately impressed. It was furnished with a double bed, a wardrobe, small desk and chair, and bedside table. It also had a sink against one wall with a small stand next to it for toiletries and towels. Next to it was a door and when Cary opened it she stood back surprised. "An indoor toilet? A shower? I certainly didn't expect this!"

"Most of our guests will be from England or the States and we felt it was worth it to pay the extra for a septic system just to keep them more comfortable. They usually have many cultural adjustments to make, and are going to be here a short time. We wanted to reduce their anxiety." She nodded a bit towards the door. "And if they don't have to go outside in the middle of the night to use the latrine, that should help."

Cary rolled her eyes and said, "You know it will! That's always been one of my biggest challenges. When James and I stayed in the Nakulabye slum, the only option was the latrine. And in the middle of the night when dog packs were scrambling, howling and fighting sometimes right next to the house, it was downright scary."

Adhe shook her head and patted Cary's arm with compassion. "We don't have running water in here, yet, so you will have to use these buckets of water for washing," Adhe said, as she pointed to buckets next to the sink, "and those are for flushing." Adhe gestured towards the bathroom and Cary saw two buckets of water back by the toilet stool. "There is bottled water in the wardrobe for drinking and brushing. When you want to bathe, let us know and one of the girls will bring you a pot of hot water."

"I love it! This is *far* better than I had expected," Cary said. "I'm sure I'll be very comfortable."

As they walked towards the house, Cary said, "I'm excited to go into your home and see what you've done. Knowing you, I'm sure it will be decorated beautifully. And I'm also sure it's been a dream-come-true to have your own house and land."

"Oh, it is!" said Adhe. "We have not had the money to do much yet, but it will be finished little by little."

When Cary walked in the door to the living room, she smiled. "Oh, Adhe. This is wonderful. The bright blues and browns in the cushion covers look so rich. And such nice photographs—I bet Sam took those. He's so good with a camera." She looked around a bit. "It's so comfortable and peaceful."

"I hoped very much that you would like it. I finished hanging the pictures only yesterday."

They walked into the kitchen, and Adhe gestured towards three women moving between the outside cookhouse and inside. "The ladies, who help us when guests come, have been here today preparing dinner. We are going to eat much earlier than usual tonight, for you, of course. We know you will want to go to bed and we also know that you would *not* be able to wait until ten or eleven o'clock to eat, as we usually do."

"Yes. Both of those points are true. I expect to be in bed by 9:00, and I've never done well with your Ugandan eating schedule."

While Adhe and Cary were talking, Mary and one of the visiting helpers had set the table for dinner. When everyone was seated, Sam prayed. "Dear Father, we thank you especially tonight that Mom has arrived safely from the States. And, dear Father, we miss our Dad, James, who is with you in heaven. Adhe and I look forward to seeing him again when *we* are in heaven. We thank you, too, for your provision of food. You are so faithful to us and we love you. In Jesus' name, amen."

The three of them had tears in their eyes, but they couldn't help but smile at the thought that they'd all be together in heaven one day, and would see James once more.

Dinner was stewed chicken, matooke³, buuga⁴, and a fruit plate with pineapple and the small "pigmy" bananas Cary loved. They also had Cary's favorite drink, passion fruit juice.

After they'd finished, Sam fired up his computer. Cary had brought a couple CDs from home, one full of photos of her new home, her family and church friends, and a music CD James had recorded with some friends. They all enjoyed listening to the music and looking at the photos as Cary described them. Cary suddenly missed James very much, and she, a "story teller", started talking.

"This one is really nasty," said Cary, winking at Adhe. "I don't know if you heard this, but after we had returned from a vacation to the house at Katalemwa, I started to wash my hands and the water smelled bad. The three of us had returned with friends from a holiday at Sipi Falls, and James hadn't even come into the house, but after dropping off Sam and me, he left town with Paul and Jodene to help them with a building project for a couple of days. There was no way to reach him, and I couldn't do anything about the house water, so I just used the filtered water we had available. Three days later, when he got home, he checked things out and discovered a bat had died in the interior water tank and had disintegrated. It was awful!" They all shuddered. "When James looked inside, the water was black and the smell was terrible. Sam and James had to clean it out by filling bucket after bucket with the black, grungy, stinky muck. Sam was the one in the attic dipping the buckets and handing them down to James. Then they scrubbed the tank with Jik[5] and water before letting it refill. Even though Sam was our house and yard helper, and was expected to do whatever we needed, we definitely gave him a bonus for that job." Cary stopped and patted Sam's arm with affection. "His willingness to take on such an awful job that made us love him even more."

Mary, Adhe, and a couple of the ladies who were cleaning the kitchen, shook their heads and made exclamations of disgust. Bats, mice, rats, and even snakes, in the wells or rain barrels were something all of them had dealt with at one time or another.

Cary continued, "After that, we repaired the protective cover over the tank." Then she laughed. "Oh, sorry to take so much of your time, but another bat story. A week or so after the water tank incident, both James and I had malaria. We were so sick we could hardly move. A bat got into our bedroom and landed on the floor and kept squeaking and brushing its wings against the floor and bouncing around. James didn't have the strength to take it out, so he crawled into the bathroom, took a small plastic wash basin and managed to plop it over the bat. But the bat scooted the basin across the floor and the squeaking and scraping were driving us nuts. James crawled out of bed again and pushed the basin out into the hall and closed the door. We could still hear the noise, but not as loudly, so it didn't bother us. The next morning when Sam came in from his quarters, he took the bat away. We kept Sam busy with lots of 'normal' work, but taking care of us during the malaria episode and rescuing us from bats seem to be the main stories I remember when I think of those days."

Sam laughed quietly. "James was a wonderful father to me. He taught me so much about videos and computers especially." He stopped and smiled. "He also taught me how to treat a wife—by watching him both here and when I lived with you in Omaha."

Adhe smiled sweetly at him and said in Cary's direction, "Dad taught Sam very well; I have a most wonderful husband."

Cary nodded. "I agree. It's very gratifying to see. And I also agree that James was truly a terrific husband."

After talking about James, Adhe said, "Mum, I think you need to go to bed." Turning to her little one, she said, "Stella, give your grandmother a hug goodnight."

Stella stood in front of Cary with a very serious look on her face. When Cary held out her arms, Stella walked closer and allowed herself to be lifted onto Cary's lap. "She's still not too sure about me," Cary laughed. "I'm sure we'll get past this."

Adhe said, "She's seen many pictures of you and your family. I think she needs a little time to put the photos and the real person together."

Cary smiled. "It's OK. I'm certainly not offended. The fact that she doesn't burst into tears every time she looks at me makes me feel pretty good. Besides, I don't know how many African youngsters her age have a white grandparent. Could be a bit of a shock."

"She sees a lot of white people from the States and England, mostly ones who come for short building projects. She probably hasn't figured out how Sam's *Ugandan* mother can be a 'grandma' and *you* can, when you don't look the same." Adhe winked at Cary and patted Stella's head while she spoke.

Cary gave Stella a hug and kissed her cheek. "Maybe you can show me your toys in the morning, Stella. I will read you a story." As Cary put her down and stood up to head to the guest house, she smiled at Stella. "We'll do fine." Suddenly Cary yawned. "But I obviously need to put my head on a pillow."

"I forgot to mention earlier. The guest house doesn't have electricity. Mary will walk you out. Oh, and there's one torch[6] by the bed in case you need a light during the night. There's another one by the sink."

"Thank you," said Cary. "I'm sure I'll be just fine." She hugged Adhe. "I love you, dear," she said. "It is so good to be here with you."

1."Ki" is "Ch", so Kiwoko is pronounced "Chiwoko".

2.People, especially young ones, refer to adults with a respectful title. Aunt, Uncle, Grandmother, etc., are the common ones.

3.Steamed green banana or plantain.

4.A vegetable similar to spinach and/or beetroot leaves.

5.Main brand of bleach.

6.Flashlight.

JOANNE NORTON

CHAPTER THREE

After Mary walked her out and said goodnight, Cary began to get ready for bed. Earlier, when she had arrived, Cary had changed out of her jeans and shirt and put on a light cotton dress. Now, she slipped out of it and changed into the nightdress Alison had loaned her. Then she brushed her teeth, washed her face, climbed under the mosquito netting, tucking it carefully between the mattress and bed frame, effectively creating a protective cage, and lay on top of the sheet.

It was a hot night. With the mosquito netting cutting back even the little bit of breeze that was coming through the window screens, Cary was very uncomfortable. She also, however, was so exhausted that in a short time she fell asleep.

Cary woke up a few hours later. Wide awake. She looked at the bedside clock and groaned. "Three-thirty AM?! *Uhh*!" moaned Cary. "I really hoped I was going to avoid this."

Jet lag always hit her. The first two or three days in Uganda, and the first week after returning home, she slept and woke at all the wrong hours of the day. "Well, the sun won't be up until 6:00 or so, so I've got a long stretch of lying here." She got out of bed long enough to get a book from her backpack, crawled back under the netting and took the flashlight to read. This worked for a while, but her eyes could only handle the dim light for so long, so in less than an hour, she was forced to lay the book aside.

A rooster crowing, loudly, startled Cary out of sleep. "I must've dozed," she thought. She looked at the window and saw dawn's pale light beginning to peek through the trees. "It'll be an hour or so before Sam's family is up and about, so I'll take a walk and make myself feel even more at home." Cary normally wasn't an early riser, if she could avoid it, but she loved Ugandan sunrises. Unlike the sunsets that fell suddenly and quickly, the sunrises took much longer and the sky was streaked with gorgeous golds and pinks and charcoals. Cary had more photos of sunrises and flowers than anything else. Her kids looked at her pictures and always asked, "Where are the people?" She never had a good answer for that— except that she loved sunrises and flowers.

Cary brushed her teeth and dressed. She was actually glad she had the sweater from the States. Early morning could be a bit chilly, even on the equator. Wearing Alison's lightweight blue cotton dress, and her own baggy black zippered sweater and high-topped hiking shoes, she had to laugh at her appearance. Her daughter would have been appalled. "Dorky" is probably the word that would have leapt to Sue's lips. However, not certain what the paths would be like, Cary didn't want to wear only sandals and was grateful to have the heavier footwear for her first venture outside.

It had been five years since Cary had walked the hills near Kiwoko. In fact, their previous home had been another couple miles further down the main road, so she knew she would need to concentrate carefully on the paths. The morning was cool and dewy and the grass and brush were saturated. As Cary passed along the narrow paths, her dress became wet from the hem and up to her knees, slapping against her legs, clammy and uncomfortable. She assumed that if she kept heading down the hills she would eventually find the main road, so that was her plan.

After walking for about twenty minutes, she realized she'd taken a wrong turn somewhere along the way. All the palm trees and banana groves began to look the same. She rounded a bend, and found herself nearly nose-to-nose with a small herd of long-horned cattle. The cattle herder, a young boy of about ten, hardly looked at her, concentrating on prodding the cattle with his stick. Cary didn't trust that the cattle wouldn't be spooked by suddenly having someone on the path. She instantly recalled the time Sam had been on a taxi with a man who had been gored in his side by a bull. The man's brother was using the taxi as transportation to get the victim to the hospital. It had not been a pleasant experience for Sam, the man, or the other fifteen passengers crammed into the over-stuffed vehicle. Recalling this, Cary quickly stepped back to give the cattle plenty of room to pass.

Cary had barely come through *that* surprise when she came across three night watchmen on their way home after working a dusk-to-dawn shift, probably for the local hospital. The watchmen looked very formidable, dressed head to toe in black, each carrying a body-length bow and a quiver full of lethal-looking arrows. Cary smiled at them and shrugged as she tried to scoot around mud and manure patches in the path. The men laughed at her. Cary knew they wouldn't know enough English to give her directions back to Sam's, so she just kept walking. She did have to chuckle, though. She remembered the first time she saw a watchman. It had been dark and she and James were walking across from their host home to a guest house during their first visit to Uganda. Suddenly, looming up in the dark was what looked like a scarecrow, which was startling enough. Then the "scarecrow" moved. Cary jumped a mile, screamed, and ducked behind James, who himself was scared silly. A couple of seconds later, the property watchman silently passed them as if they didn't exist. With today's event she suddenly realized how much Ugandan life had changed over the past several years. None of the four of them had freaked out during this sudden encounter. Even at that, she was pretty certain that running into a white woman wandering the paths in these backwoods areas of Uganda this early in the day would give them something to talk about over breakfast.

After wandering along the paths for another quarter hour, Cary began to feel nervous. This area had very few homes and, although she could hear people inside the mud-packed walls, she couldn't see any movement outside. She wasn't comfortable enough to knock on a door.

Cary was walking slowly, praying, when suddenly she heard a bicycle behind her on the path. She stepped aside to give the bike space to pass, and as the cyclist glanced at her, he fish-tailed to a muddy stop, exclaiming, "Aunt, Aunt, you have come!"

Cary laughed and reached out to grab his arm. "Alex! My heavens, it's so good to see you."

Cary and James had met Alex when they lived at the nearby orphanage and needed someone to hand-pump their water from the cistern under their porch to the water tank at the top of their house. After word spread that Cary and James were looking for help, Alex showed up on their porch, his huge smile and bright eyes contrasting greatly with the burn scars on his face. He was also missing all the fingers of his left hand. Cary and James had heard Alex's story even before they met him.

According to the story, when he was about five years old, he was pushed into a cook fire at his grandmother's. His burns were terrible and he was dumped at the hospital in Kiwoko. The nurses and doctors took him into their hearts, and provided all they could for him. Unfortunately, they weren't able to save his hand and had to amputate the fingers. Rejected by his family because of the serious needs from his injuries, when he was healed enough to live away from the hospital, he was taken to that orphanage where, years later, he came in contact with Cary and James. They weren't sure at first that he would be able to handle the job, but gave him a chance, and Alex proved to be a hard-working and faithful young man. In the six years since she'd seen him, his shoulders had broadened and he'd grown several inches, but the smile and bright eyes hadn't changed a bit.

"Auntie," he said, with concern in his voice, "why are you out here? Why are you not at Uncle Sam's?"

Cary laughed and shrugged her shoulders. "Well, Alex, I should be. But, I came for this walk and I have become lost."

"Oh, Aunt! You are so funny," Alex grinned. "Do not worry. I will take you."

Alex had two huge jackfruits strapped to the back of his bike, and immediately started to take them off. Cary tried to stop him. "Alex, you can't do that. Let me walk beside you."

"No, Aunt. Is OK. You are not far. I will put them under the tree and come back. You ride."

Cary sat gingerly on the back of the bike. Her clothes were already very dirty. She was sure this ride was going to make the clothes much worse, splattering mud and muck as Alex pedaled through the puddles and along the paths. Looking around her, holding onto the bicycle seat with an iron grip, Cary felt like she was a contestant in a reality TV show, and she wasn't doing very well at the moment.

While Cary concentrated on keeping her balance, Alex moved along confidently. In fewer than ten minutes, taking paths Cary knew she hadn't been on, Alex pulled into Sam's yard. Adhe was returning to the house from Cary's room, and rushed to Cary and Alex.

"Mum, where did you go? I found that you were not here!" She looked worried and a bit frightened.

"Sorry to scare you, dear. I just decided I'd take a walk, and, unfortunately, I got lost. And then, as I was really nervous, Alex came by. Is that God or what?" Cary ended with a laugh.

Adhe smiled. "You look as if you need to bathe. I will send Mary with hot water."

Cary peered down at the skirt of her dress and spread it out for a clearer view. "Pretty bad. I'm sorry to say, but when Mary brings the water to me, I'll give her the dress. I like to do my own laundry, but I'm going to impose on your family this first time."

"That is good. Our helper will come this morning to do our wash. Your dress should be dry by noon."

Adhe turned to Alex. "Thank you for bringing Mum home. Would you like to stay for breakfast?"

Alex smiled. "No thank you, Aunt. I left jackfruit by Kayanja's bananas. I need to go get."

Cary hugged him. "Thank you, dear Alex, and God bless you. He sure brought you to my rescue this morning."

"You are most welcome, Aunt," Alex said. "I will come again to see you."

Alex left on his bike and Cary took Adhe's hand and walked up the path. "I'm so sorry I frightened you. I really didn't think I'd get lost. However, if I'd *thought* I was going to get lost, I wouldn't have gone, right?"

A few steps later, Cary stopped and looked intensely at Adhe. "Surprisingly, Alex didn't ask where his Uncle James was, and I didn't bring it up, because he'd be so sorrowful and I'd have teary eyes. You two can tell him sometime that James is in heaven. That might be better."

Adhe nodded. "I understand."

"Thank you, honey." She kissed Adhe's cheek. "I'll get out of these messy clothes and wait for the water. See you in a while."

CHAPTER FOUR

An hour later Cary walked into the house. She looked much better than she had when she arrived from her morning's adventure. Dressed in Alison's denim skirt, a yellow shirt, and sandals, she felt a lot better, too.

"Good morning again, Adhe," she said. "Now I feel right at home. After my jaunt, I'm a little tired, but I'll try to hold out for a nap until after lunch. That way, I can help my body clock adjust to the time difference. I'd really like to sleep later tomorrow; three-thirty AM was simply too early today."

"For breakfast we have pineapple, chapati[1], and tea. Are you hungry now?"

"I'm starved! It smells wonderful." Cary looked around. "Is Sam here?"

"He left for Luweero for supplies for the children's homes. He will back at noon."

"Where's Stella?"

"Sam took her to the pre-school in Kiwoko. Even though she is only two-and-a-half years old, she loves school. It's very funny to watch her dress in her uniform. She acts so grown up. The pre-school was started recently and I'm very happy for it."

Adhe carried breakfast to the living area and placed it on two small tables, one for herself and one for Cary. Cary settled back onto the couch with her plate in her lap. Between mouthfuls she said to Adhe, "We didn't take time yesterday to talk about your work. My brain wouldn't have been able to absorb the information, anyhow. But now I want to know everything."

Adhe set her breakfast aside, and sat towards the front of the chair. She was usually sweetly quiet, but as she talked about how she and Sam had begun to dream of this ministry and how God answered their prayers, she became very animated.

"We had been with Blessing Children's Orphanage for five years, as you know. Sam worked in many positions for them, including office and personnel management. He appreciated what he had learned, but he felt he wasn't doing enough directly with the children. We had taken several children into our home for various lengths of time—such as Mary—and Sam was concerned that his duties kept him too busy to be a proper father to these children."

Adhe took a break to bring more hot water from the kitchen and replenish their tea.

"Five years ago, when Julie and Matt came from Washington state to teach and work with the construction program, we became friends. A couple years ago we began to share with them about our dream of this ministry. Did you meet them, Mum?"

"Yes, James and I met them when we were here for your wedding. They are a terrific couple. So, what did they do?"

"They listened to us and prayed with us. When they returned home, they spoke to their church. That church decided to support us while we looked for land and collected the materials for the house and other buildings."

"I know a bit of that from our phone calls and emails. I was so excited when I heard they had adopted your project. It's something James and I would have wanted to do, but we simply didn't have the funds. Nor did we have the church connections to bring this to pass. We felt pretty frustrated."

"We knew how much you would want to help. We knew you were praying for us and would support us any way you could. Loving us is enough."

Cary looked into Adhe's eyes and quietly enjoyed a moment of love. Then she said, "I am grateful that so many have now entered your life and ministry. And, I believe I do know your plan, but I'd like to hear it from you."

"Although the orphanage was doing well at caring for the children, we had a different vision. Instead of building group homes for the children, with one or two adults to live with them, we wanted to put the children into actual homes in the local villages and then help support them and the families. As you know, because of AIDS and the civil wars, sometimes there are very few adults available. We thought that if we could keep families together that were already functioning, but struggling, and if we could provide the extra provisions to meet the needs, it would be less expensive than building new places. That is how we started.

"We had three local children who had lost their parents and were qualified for an orphanage, but we found out they had relatives in the area. We went to those relatives who already had several children to care for and asked if they would take in one more child. In return, we agreed to provide school fees for the child and health care for the family if they went to Kiwoko Hospital or the Luweero clinic. If a serious emergency occurs or extra care is needed, we would contact our supporters to help, if possible, of course, but we didn't tell them that. We also offered to help them determine a money-making project that would work for them, such as raising chickens for meat or eggs, or raising pigs, or purchasing a goat or two so they could sell the milk. We pay school fees for the child we are supporting, but we also offer practical training for other children in the home. As you know, Sam is very good with computers, so he teaches a few of them the basics. Even without schooling beyond the primary level, some can learn how to run one. Sam is also good with agriculture and yard care."

Cary interrupted. "I sure know that one. I remember how amazed I was to come home and find he had pruned our mimosa bush and woven the branches together at the top and formed a crown. It was lovely. And he also took care of our vegetable garden. I was a pretty spoiled muzungu. But I loved it."

Adhe smiled. "Yes, he knows very much. So he oversees those two programs." She paused to take the dishes back to the kitchen. When she returned she continued.

"We hire others in the community to train and follow up with the families, since Sam doesn't have time to do it all. I teach the young ladies host services for guest houses, including cooking and cleaning for tourists. We don't have a public guest house yet, but we hope to have one soon. My friend Grace teaches tailoring. All of this is very basic. As you know, it is not very expensive to live out here in the bush, and we don't want to make them materialistic; we simply want them to have enough and to have the skills to support themselves if they move to Kampala or another city. Of course, the main criterion is that the family be active Christians. Right now, we have placed eight children. And we have a waiting list."

"That is so exciting. This is exactly what I have seen as a possibility for years. Although many orphanages are wonderful, I hoped something could be done to reduce the orphanages and put kids back into the community, but with resources undergirding them and providing a way for them to prepare for their future."

Adhe smiled. "We are very happy to be able to do this. It is very hard work. I am grateful for the counseling, social work and teacher training I received earlier. It comes to my aid nearly every day. I'm happy, though, to be able to work from home most of the time, instead of being gone most of the day, as was the case before. I *do* go out to help, but I can walk to most of the homes, and I can take Stella with me when I want to. I missed her so much when I worked away."

Cary said, "I hope you will show me around either later today or tomorrow morning. So far as I know, I only have a few days with you before I head to Soroti, and I want to see everything I can. I also need to visit a few of my friends at 'Blessing'. So much to do, and so little time."

"I think tomorrow morning we can visit several of the homes. Many of the people already know you from when you lived here and most have heard that our mother was coming from the States, so they want to greet you. This afternoon, after lunch, we want to hear how God called you to Soroti and what your plans are. We wanted you to be rested before you gave us the whole story, and I want Sam to be here, so even though I am very curious, I will continue to wait."

"Sounds good to me," said Cary. "And now, my dear, I must confess that I was wrong. I can't make it until after lunch before I need to sleep. I will have about two hours before Sam and Stella arrive. I'm going to put myself to bed. One thing about sleeping this time of day—the mosquitoes won't bother me, so I don't have to suffocate under that netting." She rolled her eyes.

With that, Cary gave Adhe's hand a squeeze and headed toward the guest house.

1.Chapati — a fried flatbread, like a tortilla

JOANNE NORTON

CHAPTER FIVE

It was nearly four o'clock in the afternoon before Cary walked in from the guest house. When she walked in the door, she found that Sam had returned, and they sat down to the afternoon tea, a British custom that the Ugandans had happily incorporated into their lives generations earlier. After they greeted each other, they gathered in the living room. Stella sat in the corner of the room, looking at one of the books Cary had brought over for her and holding the baby doll in her lap, a birthday gift from Grandma who had sent it a few months earlier for her birthday.

The tea was poured and passed around, the cookies were easily within reach, and the slices of mango and chunks of pineapple were under Cary's fingers. It was well known that she loved these fruits, their glorious flavors so much better than what she found at the grocery stores at home. These were grown in the yard and in nearby plots of land.

Sam settled back with his arm around Adhe. "Mom, we have emailed back and forth about the details of your trip to Soroti. I know it has to do with the invasion by the LRA[1]. However, I don't recall that you explained why you chose to do this." He grinned. "You once said that you never planned to go to Soroti under any circumstances and you didn't sound like you would change your mind on that topic. So…?"

Cary grinned back. "You're right. It hadn't even crossed my mind. Remember when Ron and Shirley asked James and me to consider going to Soroti to start a secondary school for them?" Sam nodded. "As much as I appreciated and respected them and their ministry and absolutely loved them, which I still do, I said we wouldn't. I didn't even take the time to pray about it. I wasn't going to go so far away from an international phone connection, because

35

taking a bus or taxi sixty miles to Mbale to make a call to my kids was more than I could handle. I also didn't want to deal with the dry and dusty scenery when I loved the palm trees and banana groves and flowery bushes in this part of the country. So, I turned it down flat and never regretted it."

"If you hadn't, I wouldn't have been able to go to the United States to live with you and Dad, and attend college and gain the skills I've used here to take care of the orphans, so I'm grateful you made that choice." He paused. "However, now you're here and going to Soroti. You're a very careful and practical woman. I've known you for nearly ten years and have almost never questioned that. So, how did you make this decision?"

Cary smiled and began. "I had two dreams." Cary watched their faces. Adhe looked shocked, and Sam looked a bit startled. "See, kids? That's why I didn't tell you before. I figured you'd wonder if I was on some type of drug that had affected my brain. But, dreaming, not drugging, *is* how it happened. Let me tell you the whole story, OK?"

Sam and Adhe nodded their heads and seemed to take her seriously.

She settled back comfortably with the cup of tea in her hand and a plate of fruit and cookies on her lap.

"First, I had been asked by Pastor Max to consider coming to Soroti through the organization called FAITH. I wasn't sure if this would be a God-job for me, because I didn't like what I knew of Soroti, and dealing with LRA seemed too heartbreaking. Well, when trying to decide I was grabbed through the dreams.

"That first night I had the dreams. I've never told anyone about the first one—you'll be the first to hear it. In it, I was walking through an area that I now recognize to be a street near the taxi park in Kampala. At the time, the picture didn't quite connect for me, but I knew I was in a fairly crowded location. James was walking behind me, but I didn't see him, just knew he was there. Suddenly, I came upon a big garbage dumpster. It was filled to the top, and overflowing a bit. And lying on top was a gray cat, sprawled on its back. It was scruffy and the fur was all matted and filthy. And it was wounded. It appeared to be dead. But as I watched, its eyes opened and it looked at me very intensely and I felt absolutely overwhelmed with the need to care for this cat. As I was trying to determine what I should do, I said over my shoulder to James, 'I'm sorry to have to do this, because I know you are allergic to cats, but I have to help it.' Then I found a very large towel and carefully wrapped the cat in it so that it would not be able to scratch and bite me if it tried to. My intent was to take it to a vet, since I'm not a medical person. Right after wrapping it, the dream ended.

"When I woke up, I shuddered and I went back to sleep and then this other dream hit me. What I had seen were villages in flames, children running in panic from men with guns and machetes, parents frantically searching for children. And as they passed, their eyes, all of their eyes looking at me, and seemed to ask, 'Will you come? Will you help us?' Then the scene changed to a town with long lines of people waiting for food and water. Suddenly all of them turned to look at me and said, desperation in their voices, 'Please come. Please help us.' I woke up at 4:33 and knew I must go to Soroti.

"The next day, I pulled up my emails and there was a report from 'Blessing' with the information of what they had experienced while ministering to the IDPs[2]. While reading the email, I was overwhelmed with the same emotions I felt when I woke from the dreams. And, instantly, I knew that God had dropped this into me. So, that's where it all began. And now I'm sitting here in your living room, drinking tea, eating cookies, and relishing the warmth after leaving the cold weather at home. I never would have thought my life would go this direction. Obviously, it has."

Sam and Adhe sat quietly. Finally, Sam said, "I can't help but agree with you that this was a call from our heavenly Father. *And* our father, James, would honor that call and bless you and send you to us. I think this is the time to pray."

They all moved close together and held hands, even calling for Stella to come over to them. Sam prayed. "Our dear Father, thank you for sending Mom over to Uganda to serve you and help those who are suffering and struggling in Soroti. As you have opened the doors, please help us all see what the next steps should be. Also, please surround her with your presence as she seeks your will and your protection. We bless and honor you and thank you in the name of your Son, our Lord and Savior, Jesus Christ."

1.LRA – Lord's Resistance Army

2.IDP – Internally Displaced Persons

CHAPTER SIX

Sam opened the car door for Cary. "Sorry to have to leave now, Mom. I know you don't like to start so early, especially since you hardly slept, but we need to leave now so I can be back before night." He put her large duffle and backpack into the back seat.

"I'm not upset at all. In fact, now that I will see Soroti within hours, I'm pretty excited. And I'm very grateful that you are able to take me there. I was concerned I'd end up taking a bus from Kampala, which is the worst possible option I could have faced." Then she grinned, "Well, *except* riding in the open back of a truck and that could be much worse! And without you or another friend, I wouldn't know what to do when I reached Soroti. You're a huge help." When she looked again at the bags that Sam had to put in the car, she said, "And I'm sure sorry the duffle's so heavy, but so glad all the baggage and boxes arrived."

It was five in the morning and the sun wouldn't begin to rise for another hour. Driving along the roads before sunlight was challenging. Sam and Cary needed to be on alert at all times for a number of reasons. Sometimes robbers would ambush at a junction or would set people up by putting a "wounded" person in the road and then attack the Good Samaritans who stopped to help. Sometimes animals would suddenly appear and the car couldn't stop in time—and often, if an animal was wounded or killed, even if the owner had pushed it out onto the road in front of the car so it would be struck, the driver would be forced to pay a "replacement" fee or could even be arrested by the local police for being reckless, unless, of course, the driver was willing to pay a bribe. Without streetlights or any painted lines on the roads, it was often very difficult to see, and the many potholes added to the danger.

The worst thing, in Cary's opinion, was the occasional python or puff adder stretched across the road. Driving over a large snake not only generated a bump, but sometimes the snake would to flip up onto the car hood or flit around the windows. Cary was terrified of snakes—even of the garter snakes in her yard at home—so seeing a live python or other huge snake, practically eyeball to eyeball, was very frightening.

They reached Luweero at about five-thirty and headed south to Kampala on the main highway. Sam concentrated on driving; Cary dozed in and out. Usually she and Sam talked incessantly—or, at least, *she* talked and Sam listened. They'd covered lots of territory over the last few days, so it was reasonable to relax. She certainly could trust his driving and his wisdom when it came to watching what was happening. She had to smile. When she and James moved into the house in Katalemwa outside of Kampala, Sam "came with the house." He was the yard, house, and security help. He used to go downtown with Cary to do the grocery shopping and they would carry the bags together, sometimes walking a couple miles from downtown to Wandageya where they would catch the public taxi. More than once he casually suggested that they walk off the main road and take a side street and she assumed it was just "because". When this topic came up much later, he grinned and told her it was because he knew there was trouble in the area ahead and they needed to avoid it. He didn't want to risk her being attacked or their shopping items being stolen.

This morning, to avoid the rush hour traffic, Sam took the streets that went around the east side of Kampala. Cary wasn't familiar with most of it. She saw lots of wealthy neighborhoods and the occasional slum, the two extremes usually within a very short distance from each other. About seven o'clock, Sam got on Jinja road, the highway that they would follow all the way around to Soroti, about one hundred and fifty miles. In the U.S. area, that could be covered in about two or three hours. Here it would take at least four hours, possibly five. Not only was the speed limit lower than highways at home, but the various hindrances, natural and otherwise, would slow down the journey.

Cary always enjoyed the ride between Kampala and Jinja. As they were driving past the Mabira forest Cary perked up. "Sam, did you ever talk about the forest with Fred Mukasa?"

"No. Usually we simply talk business or about the Lord when we are together."

"Last time we visited, he told me that during the Amin times and the Obote civil war, hundreds and hundreds, or thousands, of bodies were dumped in this forest. Off and on over the years since then, when driving down this highway, people have seen a woman walking across the road, usually in the middle of the night, and they've slammed on brakes, causing accidents, or driven off the road to avoid her—and then she disappeared. A ghost. Fred said he actually saw that not long ago. He wasn't the driver, just dozing in the passenger seat. The driver hollered, slammed the brakes and swerved the car, and they nearly rolled. Fred saw this woman, too. And he saw her disappear right before his eyes. I've known Fred from his church since our first visit here in '91, and I trust him. He's a very strong Christian, and for him to tell that story makes me think that what people are seeing is the truth."

Sam said, "I've heard those stories many times, of course. With all the murders and witchcraft from those years, and the rituals done to bring people partway back to life, I can see how it would happen."

"I followed the news sometimes and the number of accidents—and frequent deaths as a result—is mind-blowing."

"People are praying all over this area of Kampala, Jinja, and other towns and villages seeking God's forgiveness for these hundreds of crimes that were committed and asking him to restore and redeem the communities and families that were damaged, even totally destroyed. We're gradually seeing positive results." He paused. "And, even though that demonic spirit is seen along this highway, we know that, with prayer, the day will come when the Holy Spirit cleanses this area and that danger will be gone."

Cary patted Sam's arm. "I agree. I know the Lord is the only answer. It's true in so many circumstances in all of our lives. I can hardly wait to see Uganda restored.'

They stopped chatting after that for another stretch of time. The light was increasing, as was the traffic. Suddenly they were crossing the bridge in Jinja by Owens Dam at the beginning of the Nile. Cary shook her head. "Did I tell you the story about the guy we met at the church in Jinja during our first time here?"

Sam shook his head. "I don't think so. What was it about?"

"Emmanuel was a godly man, but he had a very bad experience during the civil war. Bodies piled up at the base of the dam, and the army moved them and usually dug mass graves. The rule was that the folks walking across the bridge to get from the cotton factory on the west side to the Jinja side could not look over the side of the dam. One day Emmanuel broke that rule. He looked. The soldiers beat him, nearly killed him, and his mind has never been healed. He worships the Lord and has a true heart for God. But he has some serious physical and mental problems."

Cary paused. "I know he was badly damaged and it shouldn't be funny, but he did do something funny with me," she chuckled. "He offered to give me a monkey. He didn't have it with him, but he said would give it to me and I could take it home in my suitcase. I told him that it couldn't work that way, because I couldn't make it through customs with a monkey. I said that it would be OK to give me a *carved* monkey, but not a real one. He finally seemed to understand. Anyhow, I didn't come home with either a real *or* a carved monkey. But I have Emmanuel's name in my Bible. Proverbs 22:3." Cary turned around and dug through her backpack for her Bible. "Here's the verse: 'A prudent man sees the evil and hides himself, but the simple pass on and are punished (with suffering).'

After I reached home and was reading the Word, that jumped out at me about Emmanuel and his life."

Sam just shook his head, a very serious look on his face. "So many incidents took place like that during the wars and fights. We all lost so many family and friends. And most of the time we never knew what happened. They just disappeared. It's a miracle that Emmanuel lived. So many didn't."

JOANNE NORTON

CHAPTER SEVEN

Sam noticed a roadside vendor group and pulled over. "Breakfast time, Mom. I can't wait any longer."

"Go for it, kid," said Cary. "You know I can't risk it. I don't need to have a 'runny tummy' over this next stretch."

Sam laughed at the Ugandan term for diarrhea; it reminded him of a church service with hundreds of people where a woman publically prayed for their visiting pastor from the States, asking that his runny tummy be healed. The poor man was embarrassed at having that announced to everyone, but the church attendees hadn't even blinked, as it was such a common occurrence and prayer request.

As soon as Sam pulled off the highway, vendors surrounded the car with skewered meat, chapatis, fruit, watches, socks, handkerchiefs, underwear, sunglasses, and more. Sam opened his window and haggled for the meat. Cary didn't open her window. While Sam was bargaining for his breakfast, she grabbed her backpack and removed a bottle of orange juice, granola bars and a banana. She showed these items to the vendors so they might stop pounding on the car, but it didn't make a difference. They continued to surround the car until Sam started moving it forward, very slowly.

Finally on their way again, they headed towards Tororo, a town famous for its monolithic rock. Sam didn't stop there, and at that point the road divided, heading north towards Mbale or east towards the Kenyan border. Sam took the north road. Reaching Mbale, they pulled into a gas station to fill the tank. They used the bathrooms, and bought sodas and bottled water. The next stop would be Soroti, about sixty miles further.

"Oh, Sam, James and I were in Mbale a few times. It always was a real treat. The scenery in the general area was amazing. And you know, because you were with us that other time when we went to the Sipi Falls." Sam smiled and patted her hand.

When Sam turned north, the instant and dramatic change of the land shocked Cary. South-central Uganda has some swamps with papyrus plants, and the plains and rolling hills are covered with banana and pineapple groves, palm trees, sugar cane fields and tea plantations. She merely blinked, it seemed, and the land flattened into rocky plains dotted with scrubby trees. The hard, rocky land in Soroti obviously wouldn't support large numbers of people. The occasional circular mud hut with thatched roof sat alone in the monotonous landscape.

Suddenly the Soroti Rock appeared on the horizon. Cary took a sudden, intense breath, her eyes widening. "Oh, Sam! I'd heard of the Soroti Rock many times, and our friend Tim climbed up on it some years ago, but I had no idea how overwhelming it is. Oh, my. I hope I can see it very well, wherever I'm staying in the town. I can hardly wait!"

CHAPTER EIGHT

When Sam pulled into the Youth With A Mission (YWAM) compound in Soroti, they saw a white middle-aged lady sitting on the veranda with a book in one hand and a cup in the other. No one else was within sight. As soon as she saw the car pull in and Cary climb out, she put both items aside and stepped down, her hand outstretched.

"Hello! I'm Jill. I'm guessing you're Cary?" Cary nodded, and Jill went on. "It's good to have you finally here. Now I can breathe easier…" Then she winked, eyes sparkling. "Assuming we get along. Otherwise, we'll just have to strangle each other and call it a day."

Cary laughed. It was such a relief to see that this British coworker had a sense of humor. It would make it easier to adjust to each others' culture, and helping others and spending time together wouldn't go more smoothly.

Jill and Sam visited for a couple minutes, glad to be face-to-face, as they had set up this meeting only through phone conversations. Sam had a connection to Jill's church in England, and he knew the local Soroti pastor who knew her, so all the networking had fallen into place.

Sam smiled at Cary. "I'll help you carry your bags into your bedroom, and I may check the kitchen for some bread and tea before heading home. I have just enough time to make it, as long as I don't get caught in traffic around Kampala. The ministry here will loan you a phone and you can call or text me any time. At least that's the plan."

Cary laughed. "I can stay here and do whatever is needed. I'm certain someone here will make sure I am content."

Sam shook his head. "Adhe and Stella would be very upset if you didn't come back before too long. And I would be, too. I have already talked to the Baptist pastor, Joseph, and he will bring you to Kampala. He has some business to take care of there, so we'll work it into our schedules. I'll see you later."

Sam turned to Jill. "Thanks for spending this time with my mom. I'm sure the two of you will be greatly used by the Lord to help at this hard time here. Now, where do I take the bags?"

Jill grinned. "Actually, the room is very small. We will be in it together, so we will get to know each other more closely than we ever would have thought. So many workers are coming to help with the refugees and we have a number of orphans staying in parts of the buildings, so this was their only option. Don't worry about the bags. We can take them; you go to the dining hall. We just had lunch, and I saw there were some leftovers. Bread, tea, and even a bit of fruit should be there waiting for you."

Sam thanked Jill, took the duffle bag and backpack out of the car and grabbed his thermos. With another quick hug for Cary, he hurried towards the dining hall.

Cary picked up her backpack, and the two of them carried her heavy duffle together.

"I could have had a larger room when I first came, but it was right next to the latrine, and the wind brought in every odor. I decided a cramped space was better than a smelly one. I hoped you would agree."

"Oh, yes!" Cary said. "I have a very strong sense of smell. Enough to drive me nuts sometimes."

They walked to the sleeping rooms at one end of the compound. The concrete walls echoed, amplifying every sound—their walking, breathing, bumping the duffle bag. When Jill reached the room and opened the door, Cary was surprised, in spite of Jill's warnings. The bed was larger than an American-style twin but smaller than a double.

It was a Ugandan double, the same as Cary's bed at Sam and Adhe's, which was very comfortable for one person. She instantly imagined the challenge of two medium-sized women trying to sleep in it. It reminded her of her time in Morocco when she had shared a queen-sized bed for a couple of nights with two other ladies; it had *not* been a comfortable experience! Now she had at least a couple weeks, not nights. Cary shook her head. "Could be interesting," she mumbled.

Jill had prepared a small path between the door and the bed. A bamboo shelf unit was against one wall, next to the window. Jill already had food, toiletries, a flashlight and a small battery-operated radio on the shelves, as well as a few books. Under the bed, she had boxes of bottled water. Crammed into the corner next to the shelf unit, she had some dish soap, laundry soap, and bleach. Actually, the room was rather organized. Now they had the challenge of fitting Cary into the room.

Cary asked, "So what now? My duffle has a lot of stuff in it, because I wasn't sure if I could buy anything here. What should I do?"

Jill said, "Well, I keep my duffle between the end of the bed and the wall, and each day I take out the clothes I'll need. There's room on the shelf for a few toiletries. The rest of your pieces can be kept in your toiletry bag in your backpack, and you can keep your Bible and a couple of other books on the shelf with my books, but you might need to put the rest of your books under the bed. And your CD player and CDs. We have to do the best we can." She suddenly looked sad. "At least we have a room, are not homeless, and haven't had the rebels attack our families and murder our children. Reminding myself of that helps me keep my everyday struggles in perspective."

Cary suddenly realized that, yes, she had just walked into a new world, for better or worse, and she needed to keep her focus on the Lord.

By the time she had her belongings in place, it was around 2 o'clock. She had heard Sam drive off a few minutes earlier. She was now really, *really* where God had called her to be, not just traveling there. She was also with the person God had arranged for her to be with, even though neither of them had any idea about it until shortly before. Both called, both ready, and both willing.

CHAPTER NINE

"Let's go to the office now," Jill said. "I can give you some info and you can see how the system works. Tomorrow we can start putting the pieces in place and decide how we're going to divide up the tasks, and work it through slowly. It will hit hard on Monday. Today and over the weekend, you can adjust to Soroti and we can breathe. It takes about twenty minutes to walk from our place to the office and you will see some of what we are dealing with. We will walk through the camp you saw as you pulled in here, and through a park where children are playing and cattle are eating. You'll begin to have a feel for people's hearts. No need to dress differently, but you might want to cover your head, since this is a very hot time of day and it feels hotter here than the southern portion you've been in." She grinned. "I learned that the hard way this week," she said, and showed Cary her legs; the backs of her calves were badly sunburned.

Cary dug out her sunglasses and a ball cap. She could hardly wait to hit the streets.

The ministry compound was right next to a large IDP camp. People smiled and children ran out to look at them as they walked past. The children usually stopped right at the edge of the pathway, hesitant to get any nearer to these "strangers." Women sat under the few scrawny trees nursing their infants, the tiny bit of shade slightly cooler. Under the veranda on the nearby building, people rested on woven mats, surrounded by piles of belongings, treasures which they'd grabbed from their house or yard as they ran to escape the rebels.

Cary spoke quietly. "This is a first for me. I've seen it on TV, of course, for years in different places, but never have I seen such in-your-face sorrow."

Jill nodded. "This week, while walking through here, I've been overwhelmed day by day, wishing I could somehow turn everything around."

After cutting through the camp, they headed across the park. Jill told Cary that it had previously been well cared for, full of flowers and colors. Now, cattle wandered around, grazing and leaving manure. Kids of varying ages played soccer, the ball made from black plastic bags rolled and tied together with pieces of banana-fiber rope, with a rock inside to add weight. Cary chuckled when she saw kids using plastic bags to sled down a dirt pile. She couldn't help but laugh at a young boy clinging to a tree branch while other kids bounced it up and down, giving him a ride. Her typically loud laugh caught their attention, and they dropped the branch and ran towards her, the little one slipping off last and rushing to catch up.

Like the kids in the IDP camp, they suddenly froze in place. Cary and Jill smiled at them, then Cary turned to Jill. "Let's walk away, and I'll show you what I used to do sometimes near our house in Kampala." Jill raised her eyebrows, shrugged and followed Cary for a few yards. They could hear footsteps behind them, some rushing forward and then slowing down. There was a lot of whispering.

Suddenly, Cary jumped around and hollered "*BOO!*" The kids screamed and ran, and while she stood there laughing, they came closer, laughing too, and began to reach out their hands to her. She stretched out her arm towards them, and they slid next to her and Jill and began touching their white skin and then giggling and jumping backwards. This went on and on for a couple minutes.

Cary asked Jill, "How do we say 'hi' in their language?"

Jill said, "It's the only word I've managed to learn. It's *yoga*, the emphasis on the second syllable."

They both said, "*Yoga*," and the kids said it back and then threw in lots of other words. Jill and Cary shook their heads, shrugged and smiled, and waved 'no' with their hands. They finally indicated they had to leave and started walking away rapidly to get the point across. They knew some of the kids would be watching for them now.

As Jill and Cary walked away, Cary dug into her skirt pocket. "I'm glad I grabbed this on the way out. It's good to be able to touch and be touched by those children, but now I'm reminded of our pastor friends, Ron and Shirley, at their church on Entebbe Road. When they were done shaking hands after the service, they'd say, 'It's time to wash "Praise the Lord" off your hands'." Cary covered her hands and rubbed her arms with the sanitizer and passed it over to Jill, both happy from their time with the kids. The kids were mostly dressed in rags, had green-gunk noses and filthy bodies, but they were funny and seemingly enjoying the life they were being forced to live. Something Cary and Jill could never have imagined.

As they reached the downtown area, things changed. There were lots of small shops, and bicycles lined the corners, their riders waiting for passengers. Radios blasted, people jabbered on cell phones. Dozens of men, probably refugees, sat on a low concrete wall around the town square, watching the goings-on with a mix of anger and suspicion. A woman walking past them with ratty hair and ragged, filthy clothes picked up the extra-long shirt she was wearing and blew her nose on the hem, revealing her ponderous breasts. She looked glassy-eyed, very much in shock. Cary was very glad she was wearing her sunglasses, as her face undoubtedly showed her shock. In the half hour since leaving the compound, she had seen more than she had ever imagined. She knew for certain that she was in the right place, but she also knew she was being challenged.

Jill led Cary into the office building and they climbed the steps to the second story where the cyber-café and several aid organizations had their signs. When they opened the door to the Pastors Working Together ministry, their chins dropped. Instead of having a couple days to learn the routine, it looked like Cary was jumping into the deep end right away.

===============

Dear Pastor,

What a crazy day! I'll tell you about the trip here to Soroti when I call you, but the main thing is that I was supposed to have today, tomorrow, and the weekend to adjust to this area and make the plans. My FAITH coworker is Jill, my new friend from England. We walked into the office to check things out and it was filled with pastors. These men wanted money to cover the expenses they'd already put out during the several weeks when no one had access to the "purse." I now had access to FAITH's several thousand dollars (8 million Uganda shillings) but had not yet gone to a bank. I ran to the bank, hoping a person with access to the safe would be there (one was! yea!) and I took out 2 million Ush and went back to the office.

Here's one example of disbursement: Pastor John needed $2,200 dollars to cover salaries and transport costs, and he needed the money immediately. What is really frustrating to me is that I have questions for the outside leadership ministry about some of the expenses requested. Some are at least double what I had been led to expect. Sometimes the need is only a phone card or gas refund. But, as described, sometimes the claims are very high. I'm especially appreciative to have Jill with me, because we can ask questions and bounce ideas off of each other and make sure we are hearing/perceiving properly. I definitely feel in over my head. I did not get nearly as much training as I had been told I would.

I came across from our office to the internet office. I will be learning how to use their system. So, I am going to spend the rest of today catching up on emails, etc.—you first—and will take the weekend to line up the ducks. Hopefully, there will be some order by Monday. But since this whole project is run on crisis orientation, I will often be flying by the seat of my pants. My heart really goes out to these pastors, who have been dealing with this for a long time—about six months since Kony came through this area. We can hardly imagine what they are going through.

Well, I need to take care of some other business and then will head back to YWAM and line my life up for tomorrow.

So happy to have access to you—online, if nothing else. And please pass this on to my kids.

Thank you and bless you.

Cary

P.S. Oh, one more thing. All the pastors' names begin with or sound like "J"—John, Job, Justin, George, Joseph, and Jacob. At least "Jill" fits right in, too. If I went by my middle name, "Jo" would blend. So, I'm not a "fitter", as usual. Oh, and if James were here instead of heaven, he'd fit in, too. Oh well...

CHAPTER TEN

"Yuk!!"

Jill grinned at Cary. "Don't like it, do you?"

"Never did, but this is worse than usual."

"I don't know. I've had sweet potatoes with peanut sauce before and it wasn't too bad."

"I don't like peanut sauce, in general, but this is worse. See the greens cooked in with it? And the grit mixed in? Makes me wonder whether the greens were washed."

"If they weren't washed well, at least they were boiled for a while. So the germs were probably killed."

Cary rolled her eyes. "Sure. Most of them. James would have been pulling his hair out, even though he was nearly bald. When we lived in Uganda he made sure everything edible was washed. First, water with a few drops of Jik in it and then rinsed with filtered water. Took extra time, of course, but we nearly always were free of any stomach issues and I think a lot of it was from being so careful."

"What are you going to do for dinner? Know what we're supposed to have?"

"I haven't heard anything."

"Well," Jill said, "I saw them preparing…fish soup."

"I've had fish soup before, and I liked it." When she saw Jill smile in a teasing fashion, Cary said, "OK. What's this like that you think I won't eat it?"

"Fish soup *here* is made from the whole thing. They clean them, but then they just hack them all up, bones, head, tails and everything else and toss them into pot. Then they have rice. You know they try to get all the sand and pebbles out, but there's always some that are missed."

Cary sighed. "I won't be eating. At least my weight-loss program is in place now. What do we have in the room to eat instead?"

"Well, what you Americans refer to as 'cookies'. I also have raisins and hot chocolate packs. So…we can do that if you prefer."

"Absolutely."

Jill and Cary spent the next few hours looking over the paperwork and receipts, calculating what they would face on Monday morning.

Later, while they were sitting on the veranda nibbling on the cookies, a couple Cary had not met walked over.

Jill nodded to each one. "Cary, this is Anne and this is Allan." She continued, "And this is our new co-worker, Cary. I'm really happy you have a chance to meet during a quiet time."

Cary noticed that they were not young and certainly did not have fresh and fancy clothes. Thinking they might be interesting, she asked, "Where are you from, and how did you end up here at this compound?"

Anne smiled. "Well, we're from the London area. We've been here most of the time for the last fifteen years. We've been with YWAM here in Uganda and in surrounding countries. We were out in the bush in a village and had to come here a few months ago when the invasion began. We weren't able to bring many of our goods with us, because we left so quickly." She sighed. "I miss being up there with the families and children; we were helping with their agricultural work."

Allan jumped in. "Yes. I don't know if you were here at the right time yesterday, but I was performing surgery on a cat. We did it on a table out here in the yard, and many of the locals, especially the teens, were standing and watching." He laughed. "I always so enjoy putting on those shows."

Cary said, "So, did the cat make it?"

"Um…no. But it was dying anyway. I'd hoped to take the cysts out of its abdomen, but it had many more than I'd anticipated. It's not as if we have X-ray machines here, especially for animals. But at least she died painlessly." He chuckled. "But the watchers were amazed to see what was being done. With the invasion the entertainment has reduced significantly, so it doesn't take much to attract many viewers."

The four of them laughed and spent the afternoon getting to know each other. They discussed how the Lord had called them to Soroti and how He was using them to bless and help others.

As Anne and Allen began to walk away, Allen stopped. "I'll be doing the sermon this Sunday at the local Anglican church. It's down on the main highway and used to boast a rather fancy cathedral style, prior to the Brits leaving this area some years ago. It's not nearly the same, now. Also, many refugees have flooded the property. I'm looking forward to sharing my thoughts. Come if you'd like; it might be interesting, especially for you, Cary."

"I'll see how things play out tomorrow, but it's quite possible that I," and she nodded at Jill, "or we, can be there. Thanks for sharing. It's been fun and I've learned a lot."

Anne turned around then. "I almost forgot—we are going to Jinja in a few days and will be gone for a few weeks. There's a YWAM conference down there. We are part of the leadership. If you are interested, you can have our room. It'll have most of our belongings in it, but it's larger and has a *private bathroom*. There's no shower water available, but it includes a toilet. Let me know in a couple of days, so I can make sure you're the ones who it is given to. I can trust you to take care of our items."

When Anne and Allen were gone, Cary looked at Jill and said quietly, "*Wow!* I can hardly imagine something that nice. Room to actually move around? I love it!"

Jill said, "Me, too. The only thing I know that you haven't heard is that the rats invade more often over on that side of the compound than on ours. So, we'll just have to pray a lot and keep our eyes open. But I'm all for having that room, too. God never said life would be perfect, did he?"

"No, he didn't." Cary paused for a few seconds and then said, "But I really hope he'll be the rat catcher and I don't have to add that to my résumé."

After they'd settled in their room for the night, at about 9:00 Cary decided to shower, or at least wash. The toilet area across the courtyard was the best place since most of the leadership stayed in that part of the complex. She grabbed her towel and a long nightshirt and stepped outside. It was then that she remembered something important—the guard dogs were loose. Cary was normally nervous around dogs, especially big ones, and these were very, very big. She never had to deal with them, because they were kept in cages during the day. Suddenly she was eyeball-to-eyeball with a dog that had barked, run up to her, and plunked his paws on her chest. She was very happy to find out it was friendly. She figured that if she'd been trying to come in over the gates, it would have been a different story. Once her heart stopped racing, she backed up and he backed down. "Good doggie," she said, and walked slowly across the courtyard.

Washing was always a challenge for her. The water was cool at best, cold at worst. The pipe came out of the wall right about waist high for her, so she had to bend and squat and pour, and then hope that the water wasn't a thorough mess on the floor, since there wasn't any type of stall barrier.

Since she hadn't forgotten about the dog, she was on alert while walking back to the room. The dogs weren't startled by her and just roamed casually nearby. At least her shirt didn't end up with dirty paw prints after the shower. The light was on when she reached the room, but Jill was sound asleep. And even though it was Cary's turn to sleep on the outside of the bed, Jill had fallen asleep in that spot. Cary groaned quietly. After she dug out her CD player, put on the headphones, and turned out the light, she climbed into the bed, back against the wall. Despite her discomfort she was asleep very soon.

CHAPTER ELEVEN

Cary and Jill had risen and were dressing when they heard tapping at their door.

When Jill opened the door, Anne smiled and said, "Hi, ladies. Are you coming to the church?"

Jill grinned. "Yes! Do we walk with you or go on our own?"

"Well, Allen left a while ago to plan his sermon in the area. And he took a bike for a prop for his teaching. When will you be ready?"

Jill looked at Cary and shrugged. Cary said, "Oh, a few minutes. Just need to comb my hair and brush my teeth. We look forward to time with you."

"I'll wait for you at the gate. I'll visit with my Uganda boy who guards the property."

A few minutes later, Cary and Jill walked out, carrying their Bibles, and Anne smiled as they met her.

When they started walking a different direction than Cary was used to, she said, "In the few days I've been here, I have never walked on this main road. I've always walked through the IDP place near the YWAM or going downtown on side roads. This is much different." She glanced at Anne. "Was this where the Brits lived years ago? There are a number of special-looking houses and parks. Really looks different than other places I've seen." Cary looked impressed.

"Well, yes. When the Brits left all those years ago and the Ugandans took over, their leaders kept this special, but since the IDPs rushed in here, there's really no normal anymore." She pointed across the street, and Cary's gaze followed.

"What's going on?"

Anne grimaced. "The reason I brought us onto this side of the street because over there, the men use that huge tree as a latrine. As you may have noticed, even on this side of the street it doesn't smell very nice."

Jill and Cary smiled. Jill said, "Thanks, Anne, for helping us not be buried in lots of smelly stuff. This IDP situation has really hurt so many people. Breaks my heart."

A few minutes later they walked into the churchyard. Cary was shocked. She said, "Many people may go *into* the church, but many stay *outside* where they are camping. I should go around town more often to see these situations."

"The invasion added about one hundred thirty-six thousand people to the town, which originally only had a population of about fifty thousand," Anne said. "So it's very difficult for people to find accommodation."

They walked into the church. It was large, its walls and floor and seats looking well-worn. Cary wondered if that was only from the IDPs. A few hundred Ugandans were there. As Cary, Jill, and Anne were the only muzungus, many people stared at them.

When the pastor, Johnson, entered, he began with prayer and then spoke clearly about the necessity of having joy in the midst of sorrow and suffering. He said it was important to rely on the Lord and worship him no matter what was happening. The people nodded and agreed, even though most of them were IDPs, people who had suffered so much. After that, he led the congregation in singing. Cary and Jill were pleasantly surprised to hear and sing the Isaac Watts hymns. They rejoiced with those, but when the song "I Will Enter His Courts" began, they held their arms up high in worship and were filled with joy. They kept grinning at each other and smiling at the people, few of whom could sing in English. The music was familiar, but the wording was quite unusual. The Teso language was impossible for them to follow.

Allen was introduced as the preacher, and he surprised them when he walked up with his tandem bicycle. As he started speaking, Cary noticed that he kept his verbal pieces fairly short, which made it easier for the translator. If a Westerner wasn't used to working with a translator, he or she might speak in very long segments, which made it very difficult for the translator. Allen didn't give an introduction, but jumped right in.

"This tandem bicycle is an illustration of marriage. The man rides in front and controls the steering and brakes, but his wife is behind pedaling and sharing the work. As one or the other needs, they can take a rest and let the other pedal. But overall, it's a team effort; they share both the work and the results of their labors. Let's take an example from the Bible." He smiled. "Joseph, Mary, and Jesus were IDPs in Egypt. They needed this bike, or their donkeys, and to focus on moving forward. In our world, that's what husband and wife need to do, also."

As the sermon went on, many of the people clapped and smiled.

As people were leaving the church, Cary and Jill were visiting some of the IDPs. Allen stood with them. He pointed out one of his favorite Teso ladies, sitting on the porch. "She is a charismatic Catholic and has been in this town for many weeks, since the LRA invaded her village. She truly loves to worship, and, because she is Catholic, a non-Catholic pastor in another town told me that she really didn't know the Lord. Oh, she *truly* does. And she does so much for many, helping even though she has lost all of her possessions. He smiled at her. "Although she surely must have a tribal name, she calls herself Mary."

Cary smiled and tapped Mary's shoulder. When she looked up, Cary said, "Thank you so much for worshipping and sharing our Father." Mary smiled and nodded.

Cary and Jill looked for Anne, ready to return to the complex, but Allen intercepted them. "Ladies, we're taking you to lunch. You've blessed us to be here, so we'll try to bless you." Cary and Jill accepted, their stomachs already rumbling.

CHAPTER TWELVE

A man who oppresses the poor is like a sweeping rain, which leaves no food [plundering them of their last morsel.] Proverbs 28:3

Cary really wanted to sleep in on Saturday morning, six days after her arrival in Soroti. It had been her turn to sleep on the inside of the bed, against the wall, and she kept bumping against the wood frame on the side of the bed. Jill's position on the outside allowed a bit more space, and she was out cold. To make matters worse, the African mission student responsible for making breakfast was in the kitchen banging pans, blaring the radio, and singing off-key at six o'clock. The sun wasn't even up yet, so it was ridiculous that *he* was. The sound ricocheted off the kitchen's plaster walls, and seemingly increased in decibels as it bounced across the courtyard and through their bedroom window. Cary found it very annoying.

The night before, another student had sung and played a phrase on his guitar over and over again for an hour, oblivious to the fact that his voice was off key and the guitar was out of tune. Jill and Cary passed the headphones for the portable CD player back and forth to try to obliterate the student's efforts. When Cary was ready to scream, the student finally gave up and took his talents to another end of the compound. At any rate, Cary hadn't gotten to sleep as early as she'd hoped. In addition to the noise, the night was hot, and what little breeze there was didn't make it through the mosquito netting—unlike the mosquitos—so she felt stifled and claustrophobic.

Finally Cary had slept, and morning had come. After trying unsuccessfully to shut out the kitchen noises by burying her head under her pillow, she gave up and crawled out from under the mosquito net. She smashed against the back wall and stumbled around over the duffle bags piled at the end of the bed as she got dressed, then headed to the dining room. After all the breakfast prep with its accompanying noise, only tea, bread, and jam were set out.

"I could have accomplished this task with a lot less noise and in a lot less time," Cary mumbled. "Crashing around the kitchen at six o'clock, I could have made Eggs Benedict and cinnamon rolls. Oh, well."

At eight o'clock Cary went back to the bedroom. Jill was still sleeping. "Hey, Jill. Time to get up." Cary nudged her, and Jill opened her eyes and instantly looked all bright and cheery. "How did you manage to stay asleep with all that racket?"

Jill shrugged as she threw back the blankets. "Guess it's from living so close to noisy streets at home in Worcester. That's not as noisy as London would be. But once I am out, I am *really* out."

"Well, breakfast is on the dining room table. Plain ol', plain ol'."

Jill climbed out of bed and started digging through her duffle. "I know we're going *boda*[1] and I know the rule is for women to ride sidesaddle, but I can't do that. I'm sure I'd fall off. And I know I can't wear slacks." She kept rummaging around in her bag, and finally pulled out a knee-length garment that looked like a skirt. "But I do have this pair of culottes."

"You're kidding!" Cary said. "That's not fair. I only have dresses. I left my jeans at Sam's, because I was sure I couldn't wear them here. And *you* can ride more comfortably and safely than I can."

Jill laughed. "Some days are harder than others. Sorry, but I'm not changing my mind."

"If I'd known you were going to do this, I might have decided to hire a taxi instead of a bike." Cary rolled her eyes. "Oh, well. I'd rather wear a dress and *boda* for cheap than ride in a taxi and pay all that extra money—it would have cost several dollars to get to the children's camp three miles away. Anyway, I arranged for the young man named David to bring a partner and come here at ten o'clock."

Cary and Jill spent some time washing a few clothes and sweeping the room. Cary knew it was awfully late at night in Newton, a little after midnight, but she decided to call Pastor Max anyway. The signal was good, as usual, and the connection was clear.

"Good evening," he said.

"Hi, my friend. I'm sorry it's so late, but I wanted to check in."

"That's OK. It's good to hear your voice. How are you doing?"

"Well, we may have a hard day ahead of us. We're going to the children's camp I told you about. Hearing their stories could be pretty tough."

"I'm sure. This is a new experience for you, even with all the time you spent in Uganda before. I'll be praying for you, sharing you with the church."

"I have another challenge, first thing this morning."

"What's that?"

"I have to *boda*."

"Oh, the bike thing. You've done that before, haven't you? Why is it a challenge?"

"Previously I was out in the country with few people to see me. I was wearing jeans and sitting on it normally, as you would sit on a bike. Today I have to wear a dress and do it sidesaddle and go through the camps with people watching, and if I fall off it's going to be a hoot and it'll be told all around town that this white woman fell off a bike!"

She heard him chuckle. "Sorry," he said. "I know I shouldn't laugh. But, I'm sure you'll do fine. And, because you remember how cheap the ride is, you'll be able to pull it off with pleasure. At least that's the impression I have."

She smiled. "Here I called you needing sympathy and instead you're being practical."

"I definitely do sympathize. And, as I said, I promise to share with the church so there will be prayer for your safety and that your driver will be respectful and do a good job. And, I'm looking forward to hearing from you after you are back today. I do realize that what you're doing today might not be spread around very quickly, because of the timing, but I am going to email many of them, and they will hear the results as soon as possible. If nothing else, depending on the time, be sure and email me and I'll read it first thing in the morning before I head for church so the prayer group will have something to post."

"I will. And, it's nearly time to go, so I need to finish a couple of chores. I hope you are able to get back to sleep quickly."

"No problem. I'll pray and sleep. Greet Jill for me and tell her I'm blessed that you have a friend with you."

They both said, "Bye" at the same time, and Cary clicked off the phone and sighed heavily. She turned to Jill and gave her the message from Pastor Max.

One of the students came to their window. "Madams, someone is here for you."

David and his friend John were right on time. David greeted them very politely, although he spoke very little English. John seemed to speak none. The only real word that passed between them all was *Yoga*. The money had been arranged the day before, so for two thousand shillings, or about one dollar each, the boys would cycle them to the camp and back, and wouldn't expect a tip. Cary called this a "cheap date."

Jill showed real confidence climbing onto John's bicycle. She smirked at Cary as she tightened her culottes to make sure they didn't get caught in the spokes. Cary carefully climbed on the back of David's bike, crossed her feet onto the rod, and grabbed the hardware under the seat. Once they both seemed secure, the boys took off.

It was another exceptionally hot winter day. The first part of the ride was down a tree-lined boulevard where mansion-style houses from the British years were still in place. The shade and breeze were a big help. Earlier, while washing and hanging her clothes, Cary knew it was hot and knew she should wear sunscreen, but it was always a challenge. When she wore it, within ten minutes her face was a greasy mess, with sweat and sunscreen running into her eyes and blinding her. Today Cary decided to forego the sunscreen. Instead she had opted for a loose, long-sleeved shirt and a brimmed hat. And she prayed.

The bikes soon turned away from the boulevard and hit the side roads, which were full of potholes and bumpy ruts. Cary tightened her grip on the pieces of the bike and felt her feet trying to grip the footrest. She glanced behind her. Jill's eyes were wide, and she also seemed to be holding on tightly, obviously hoping not to end up in a ditch.

Suddenly, children started running to the edge of the camps, pointing and laughing. Their moms, sitting in the background and stirring pots on three-rock fires, looked over their shoulders and laughed, too. However, it was obvious from their tone of voice, even though Cary and Jill couldn't understand one word of it, that they were telling the kids they couldn't leave the camp and chase the bikes. That was a huge relief.

While Cary was watching the kids, she felt the bike slither. She grabbed the seat harder, then turned and saw David jerking. "Oh, no!" The bike slid, and for a split second she panicked. She heard Jill hollering, "Cary! Jump!" And she did. She hit the ground feet first, stumbled around for a couple of seconds but miraculously stayed on her feet. She hadn't fallen into the gravel or thorns just off the path.

David didn't crash the bike. He hit some sand and the bike fishtailed, whipping back and forth several times. He turned to look at Cary, wide-eyed. "Oh, Madam, sorry. Hurt?" He pulled the bike back towards her on the path.

"I'm OK, David. A little shaken up, but OK. Let me settle back on so we can keep going." In the background, Cary heard the children clapping and their mothers warbling, rejoicing because Cary had not been injured. John had stopped behind Cary and David, and when Cary turned around and looked at Jill, she was still sitting on the bike, looked like a statue, and was breathing heavily. "Glad you made it, Cary," she said. "I was very worried."

"Thanks for telling me to jump. I don't know where I would have ended up if you hadn't." Cary turned to David. "Let's keep going. We need to get to the camp."

They rode for several more minutes, and when they came around the Soroti Rock curve they saw the camp. Armed guards stood by the entrance; a long tree branch hung from the fences on both sides of the driveway, barring the way. The guards looked very serious, but when the counselor, Susan, came out and welcomed Cary and Jill, the guards moved the branch, stepped aside and nodded their permission to enter. Before walking through, Cary looked at David. "Can you come back in two hours?" David looked at John, and then nodded.

They climbed on their bikes and rode away, heading downtown. Cary looked at Jill. "I sure hope we communicated clearly. This language barrier has been a problem so many times this week."

Susan, a lovely young woman they'd met three days earlier through Pastor John, welcomed them with real enthusiasm.

"Hello. It is so good to see you. I hoped you would come and see the children."

Cary smiled. "Thank you, Susan. We have wanted to do this. If they are willing, we want to hear their stories." Jill stood beside her and nodded.

"Please come with me, and I will take you to a quiet place where you can visit easily."

As they turned to follow her, a guard called out. Cary didn't understand because he spoke in Teso, but when she saw Pastor Julius at the gate, she knew why the guard was hollering. She and Jill smiled and waved. Susan nodded and they let Pastor Julius in.

He walked up to them. "I wanted to be here on time to be an interpreter for one of you. I remembered you said you would try to be here today. Am I late?"

Jill shook her head and smiled. "You made it at exactly the right moment. Thank you for coming; I know it will make a big difference. Now we can each interview a child, Susan interpreting for Cary, and you can be with me, if that's OK with you."

He smiled. "More than happy to."

Susan began walking again. "Let us go into the girls' dormitory. It is too hot to sit on the veranda. I know it will be hot in that room, but the sun will not be shining on you."

They walked into a dorm which had previously been used as barracks for Soroti soldiers. Cary shook her head. It amazed her how they managed to get so many three-tier metal bunk beds and the small plastic washing tubs and other necessary items in this room. There were hundreds of beds, with barely enough distance between them for the girls to climb up and down. She had been told that UNICEF had provided the beds and foam mattresses, and Serve the Children-Norway had given the wash basins and blankets. The room was very basic, but the girls had a safe place to be, and these were probably better sleeping facilities than most of them had in their small villages.

Jill and Pastor Julius sat on the opposite side of the room from Cary and Susan, the chairs resting on woven banana-leaf mats on the concrete floor.

Cary heard a noise, and she saw a woman lying on a bed. She seemed to be reading a Bible, but kept making guttural sounds. When Susan returned, before Cary started interviewing the child Susan had brought in, she quietly asked about this woman.

"She is mentally disturbed," Susan said sadly. "She never moves away. During your time here, even if it is hours, sitting very near her bed, she will never acknowledge our presence and never change her position. We had not planned to support anyone this badly sick, but there is nowhere else to send her, and no family has ever come that could help." Susan sighed. "She is not the only person in the camp who is not what we call a 'rescued child'. We have young children in the camp, children who became separated from parents during the panic of running from the rebels and who have never been reunited with family. When it comes to this woman, whether she had been rescued from Kony's groups or had become lost while fleeing the village, she had nowhere to go and no one to help her. She has become part of the camp as it's a place of safety. We hope it will change for her."

When they finished talking, they turned together and Cary took a good look at her first interviewee. Susan introduced him. "Madam Cary, this is Vincent. I will tell you a little before you ask him more questions. He is twelve years old."

Cary interrupted her. "Twelve? I never would have guessed that. His legs and arms are so spindly and look like they are sprouting from his shorts and shirt. He looks like a nine-year-old boy."

Susan nodded. "I agree. However, look into his eyes and tell me what you see."

Cary stopped talking and, as Susan suggested, did look very solidly into his eyes. "My heavens! I think I am looking at a very old man." Her eyes immediately started to fill with tears and she turned her head away so he wouldn't see, pulled herself under control, and turned back again.

After writing down his name and age, Cary asked how the rebels had found him and when he had been abducted.

Vincent looked at Cary but spoke in Teso, and Susan translated simultaneously (continuously, instead of stopping and starting). He said he was from a village in Katakwi district. Susan stopped and said to Cary, "That is where most of the children come from, as I'm sure you know. In fact, that is where most of the IDPs come from. It is about twenty kilometers northeast of here." She nodded at Vincent and he continued with his story. He was not taken during the first wave of attacks, but a couple weeks later. He and his fourteen-year old sister had been sent by their parents to hide among the cassava plants near their house. The rebels found them there and tied them together. The group was small, only ten rebels and seven children.

Cary stopped him and turned to Susan. "What size were most of the groups? Was this normal?"

Susan shrugged her shoulders. "Some are small like the one he was taken with. Some have hundreds of both rebels and children. Most certainly the large ones are in places where more food and water was available. However, the war has not ended yet, so we do not have all those answers. We may know in a few months."

When she asked what he went through as an abductee, Cary anticipated that he would be nervous about giving those details. She was wrong. Vincent was very matter-of-fact in the way he described life on the run through the bush. He talked about being beaten, and showed Cary his legs and arms, covered with scars. He said, "My sister and I were forced to carry heavy loads, forced to steal, and to walk very far with very little food."

Vincent continued. He said, "In August, after only a few weeks, I was left behind. My foot was infected and swollen. The rebels had tried to clean my foot. They poured boiling water on it."

Susan pointed to his foot, and that part of his foot was red and painful looking. Cary shuddered when she saw it. Vincent said, "Because of the foot wound, I had become sick. I was not able to work for them, so they left me behind, put me off the paths under a tree. I couldn't walk and had no food or water. The rebels thought I would die, and I thought I would, too." He shook his head.

Susan said, "But he did survive. He was found after some days. They took him to a hospital in Lira, about seventy-five miles from Soroti, and he was there for about two months. His parents are still in their village, but they have come to visit him a few times. He wants to go and be with them, but he cannot because it is too risky—if he was captured again, the rebels would kill him. That is what they do to make an example of those that escape. Of course, his parents won't allow that. Once the rebel threat is over, he will be gone. And that family—and many others who finally reconnect with each other—will be very joyful. I can hardly wait."

When Cary had listened to Vincent and Susan, she asked if she could pray for him. He seemed very content with that suggestion. She reached down and took his hand, and nodded at Susan so she would interpret.

"Dear Father, thank you for this young man. Thank you that Vincent has been receiving medical help, and is eating, and is not being beaten or forced to carry heavy burdens. Thank you for rescuing Vincent and for letting him see his parents. I ask, Father, that you touch his body and bring healing to him so he will be strong. And I also ask that you touch his heart and heal it, too, from all he heard and saw during that time. And I thank you that I have been privileged to meet Vincent. In Jesus' name I pray. Amen."

Vincent nodded his head and said "thank you" in Teso. While he was standing up from the mat, and turning to the door, Susan leaned over to Cary and whispered, "His sister is still missing."

While Susan followed him out of the door, Cary recalled what she had been told earlier in the week. Most abductees who could no longer serve, or who were wounded and did not recover quickly, were killed. The rebels were concerned that if the militia or army found the child, he or she could give out information. She was happy for Vincent and she felt very blessed to meet him.

When Vincent left, Cary looked over at Jill. A teenaged girl was leaving and seemed happy. Her clothes were nice and she didn't appear to have been beaten. Pretty amazing.

Susan left for a couple minutes, and Cary wandered out near the door. She saw a teenage girl holding a large plastic cup with water. A small girl about four years old stood in front of the teenage girl, and they were looking in the door and trying to see the ladies who had come in. This little girl was wearing what had originally been a very fancy dress—a style worn to a wedding or something that special. This girl's dress was torn all the way below her neck and down to her stomach. The pieces on her shoulders were torn, too. Cary turned towards Jill and gestured towards the door with her eyes, so Jill would notice. They both were amazed at how this little girl was so happy to be wearing this worn-out, torn dress. Cary wanted to take a picture and show it to her granddaughters and others who might complain about not having enough clothes.

When Susan walked back, the two girls smiled and Susan winked at them and patted the little one on her head. They walked off.

When a teenaged girl walked into the door, Susan had Jill and Pastor Julius bring their chairs over. They introduced everyone and sat down together. Christine spoke English fairly well. She was fifteen years old and had been in a good school before being abducted. Susan said, "Christine was given to a twenty-seven year old rebel man as his third wife." Cary was shocked! Susan continued. "He had two wives and the three of them beat her and refused to give her food. One of the wives was pregnant. After a couple months of with them, she escaped during crossfire between the militia and the rebels."

After hearing this from Susan, and seeing how Christine was nodding, Cary looked at her gently, took her hand, and asked, "If you could talk to these people, what would you say?"

Christine said, "I would tell them that I forgive them, because they don't know what they are doing."

Cary was overwhelmed; she could hardly stay in her seat. She shot a glance at Susan, who nodded her head. Obviously, the response was not aimed to impress a missionary woman or aide worker. Christine's simple truth poured from her heart. Jill also seemed impressed and uplifted.

Before Christine was done sharing, they saw a teenage boy come and stand out of hearing. When Christine left, Susan and Pastor Julius warned Cary and Jill that his was a very difficult story to hear. Susan said his English name was Brian.

He said, "I was in a large group of people, and I ran away. I was able to get under trees and in a hole nearby. The men came after me with their machetes, and after a few days they got me out. They grabbed me, took me back to their group, and hit me with the machetes. They cut my back and my arms, which were very thin because of the days and weeks I had hardly eaten." He took off his shirt and stood up. It was horrible. He had many cuts from his neck to his waist. The more he talked, the more they could sense his anger. They told him he was loved. They touched him gently, and all prayed.

There were two children waiting, so Jill and Julius went back to the other end of the room. A young boy walked up to Cary and Susan. Cary's heart reached out to him, just seeing him. Elijah, ten years old, talked about the hard life and the abuse, and showed them the many wounds on his legs. When he finished and was willing to be prayed for, instead of letting her hands surround his, the normal way, his surrounded hers. As she prayed and glanced at him, tears ran down his cheeks as he pressed her hands very tightly. She longed to throw her arms around him and pull him up onto her lap, but as that wouldn't be culturally OK, she managed to hide her emotions. She knew her heart would have a memory of him forever.

After he left the room, Susan said, "He arrived here from a hospital just yesterday. We have sent a helper out to try to find his family."

Cary was glad Elijah was her last interviewee for the day. She didn't think she could any handle more at that moment.

At the two-hour point, David and John came back to pick up Jill and Cary and take them back to the compound.

After two hours of stories of rape, murder, beatings, and seeing the damage inflicted on these children's bodies and souls, Cary was thoroughly distraught. She felt blessed to hold their hands and pray for these victims. She had watched Jill question those who came to her, and saw when she appeared stressed, furious, heartbroken.

While riding on the back of the bike, she was no longer in the mood to wave to kids or anyone else near the IDP camps along the roads. Elijah's and Christine's stories continued to echo through her mind.

Cary was grateful that the bikers had arrived shortly after she and Jill had discussed each other's stories briefly. She knew it was going to be tough to really discuss them and work through them emotionally. Since Jill was a bit introverted and Cary was highly extroverted, Cary wasn't sure how it would play out, but she knew the Lord could work it through with them. It was daunting, knowing that this was only the first set of interviews. Cary wondered how she could keep doing this without crumpling to the floor. Again, she knew it was only by the grace of God that it could be done, and *she* could. She *must* trust him.

Hours later, after emailing Pastor Max, her kids, and her prayer partners, telling the stories of the eight kids she and Jill had interviewed, then having dinner with visitors at the compound and finally having "alone" time, the day's events finally hit Cary full force. As she had anticipated, but hoped wouldn't be the case, she began to cry. She picked up a book she had been reading and threw it onto the floor.

"Why, Lord? *Why?* There's no reason those kids should have to go through that. And to know some of them are Christians, and their families have been serving you, and yet they are suffering from physical and emotional beatings, forced to watch others being killed, forced to steal and beat others, the girls forced to be sex slaves. I know it's not *your* fault, but...*why?*" She collapsed onto the bed crying her heart out. Jill reached over and patted her hand. Not much else could be done.

After she stopped crying, Cary looked at Jill and shook her head. "I'm sorry. I know I shouldn't overreact like that. I know 'God is bigger'. I say it all the time. But what keeps piercing my heart is, 'How can I go back home to Disneyland?' after seeing what these innocent ones have gone through." Cary shrugged. "But I know I'm here now for a purpose, and I need to keep my eyes on the Lord."

Jill nodded. "You are right, Cary. God has us here for a reason and for a season. He will show us his purpose. It's not easy, that's for sure, but it is the right thing to do."

Soon all the lights in the compound were out, all the music was off; it was quiet. The night was cooler than usual and no mosquitos flitted through the screens. Cary and Jill fell asleep, and both of them had their best sleep since Cary had arrived.

----

1 "Boda-boda" is the Ugandan term for a common form of bicycle or motorcycle transportation. Usually, the passenger sits on a (slightly) padded saddle on the back, placing feet on the footrest, similar to a motorcycle. Locals use this transport frequently, carrying food, furniture, children, and the occasional chicken or goat.

JOANNE NORTON

CHAPTER THIRTEEN

Thankfully, Monday was a fairly slow day, with very little stress. Cary took care of the basic needs. Jill stayed at the compound until shortly after noon and came to the office so they could go to lunch. They headed to a small café, and after settling in, they saw two ladies across the porch who were obviously working with other aid groups. They asked to join them, then pulled the tables together to share stories. One of them was Kevina, a Ugandan lady whose group was helping the youngest children—those who had been separated from their family during the village invasions—to find their relatives. The other lady was from Sweden, working with UNICEF. Cary was grateful they'd ventured over to join them, encouraged by their commitment to helping the children no matter the cost.

The two ladies left, and Jill and Cary continued eating. Suddenly they heard a roar. They turned to look at the main street nearby and saw army trucks filled with soldiers, each one holding a weapon. A truck also came through with a military tank on the back.

Cary stared, smiling. "At home, our families are going about business as usual, and we are sitting in the war zone of Soroti eating hamburgers, watching soldiers with their rifles ride past in massive trucks. It's surreal somehow, but I love it."

Jill looked at Cary. "And who would have thought we would spend winter in this heat? Pretty amazing."

Cary nodded. "Did I tell you what I heard on the way to the office this morning? I was walking past shops and heard a song by an American country star from the 1950s and 1960s, Jim Reeves. The song was 'Bimbo'. Made me laugh, since I haven't heard that song since I was a kid."

"Really? I vaguely remember his name. Why would you hear it here?"

"Jim Reeves has been popular in Uganda for all these years, even though he died in 1964. Hearing his voice while walking down the street here, I nearly burst into tears. It made me homesick instantly."

Jill shook her head, overwhelmed, and stood up. "We'd better head back. Looks like we have a light day, and that's a relief." They pushed their chairs in and picked up their bags. "Did you get any emails this morning in response to what you sent out about the interviews?"

"Nothing yet. But the cyber-system has been off kilter, so I wouldn't be surprised if there are a few out there waiting to hit our inbox. My pastor and my kids haven't even been able to reach me because the phones are down so much. I have to be patient, which is really not one of my strong points."

Jill grinned. "I think I've noticed that already in our short time together."

They returned to the office and the day went on quietly. Nothing big. No pastors came around. Cary and Jill assumed it was because they were busy helping the refugees on their church grounds.

Pastor Joseph had mentioned something about this recently, and it had shaken Cary up. He'd said, "The invasion happened overnight and the 'helps' arm of the church was weak and unprepared for the crisis. We thought the 'emergency' might last for a couple weeks. Instead, it has continued unabated for six months. All of us are absolutely exhausted physically, emotionally, and spiritually. Our families are exasperated with us, upset because we rarely have family time."

That comment had resonated with Cary, and she smiled when she realized no pastors were around. It was truly a restful afternoon—for everyone.

CHAPTER FOURTEEN

The next day, Cary went into the internet office before joining Jill in the main one. The secretary waved at her as she came in. "Miss Cary, our system is working well today. You will be able to connect now."

"Thanks. I'm a very happy woman. I hope all comes through that we've been waiting for."

Cary rejoiced as she pulled up the emails. One from Sue, one from Pastor Max. Long and caring. One from Sam and Adhe. A few from people who had been touched by the interview report. Then an email from someone Cary didn't recognize. When she opened it, she realized it was connected to the Pastors Working Together ministry. It was from Kampala, and although Cary didn't recognize the name, the attachment definitely laid out what was expected of her.

"Madam, attached is a contract that Pastor Justin is to see and I desire that his comments be sent to me. Please do this as quickly as possible."

When Cary walked into the office, Jill had arrived and was unloading her case. Cary heard the frustration in her own voice as she spoke. "I got instructions on taking a document to Pastor Justin. I don't know where he is or how to reach him. As you know, he doesn't have a phone. All I can think of doing is tracking down Joseph or Jacob and see if one of them can get here in a reasonable length of time."

Jill pulled out her cell phone. "I'll call both of them and see which one can come."

An hour later, Jacob came by. Cary had been at the internet office and answered the emails, waiting for one of the pastors with the document in hand.

They climbed into his van. Jacob said, "I know where he lives, and we should be there in just a few minutes. I'm very pleased to help."

They drove along the dirt road next to several small concrete houses, most of them duplexes or triplexes, recently built since the invasion and the thousands rushing to Soroti. Cary had been told that most had only two rooms—an open room and a bedroom. The cooking area was outside on the concrete pad by the door. The community latrines were off a bit in the distance.

Jacob pulled up alongside one of the homes, recognizing Pastor Justin's bike leaning against the wall.

When they reached his door, Pastor Justin came out and greeted them both very warmly. This dear pastor, someone Cary had come to respect and love almost instantly when she first met him, was about sixty years old, could barely read, and did not drive. He had pastored in the villages surrounding an area that was invaded. He had no family with him, but he'd been given a house because he so often had others staying with him and he was known as a kind and loving man. His Pentecostal church was being built only a few hundred feet away.

Cary smiled and held his hand momentarily. "Pastor Justin, I received this document from Pastor Godfrey in Kampala. He wants you to sign this. I know you probably can't read the whole thing, but Jacob can read it to you. It should only take a few minutes. Then I can have it scanned and sent to him."

Justin looked at the two pages and squinted a couple of times, then said, as he handed the document to Jacob, "I can read *some* of the words, but I do not see well lately and can not purchase glasses. Please..." he said, as he motioned to a bench.

Jacob sat on the bench and began to read. While the two men sat focused on the papers, Cary decided to wander around. Everyone stopped and stared at her; they rarely saw white people in their area, especially those who had been living in the villages. She was a whole new experience for them.

Cary suddenly noticed a young child lying on a straw mat on the cement pad outside Justin's house. At first, she assumed the girl was sleeping, although she wasn't sure why she would be outside. When Cary looked closely, she saw tears on her cheeks.

She interrupted the pastors. "I noticed that little girl is crying. Can you ask why?"

Jacob set the papers aside and walked to the mother, and the two of them spoke for a short time. Jacob turned to Cary. "They were heating water in a kettle on their three-rock fire, one of the rocks shifted, the kettle hit the floor and boiling water splashed on the girl's neck, shoulder, and chest. It happened not long before we came. She is in great pain."

"She's hardly crying, though. If that happened to one of my grandkids, they'd be screaming their head off. Why isn't the family doing anything?"

"In our culture, if a child is hurting, it is right to be as silent as possible. One reason is because our people are so poor they can't afford to go to a doctor. In fact, one is rarely around. So, they simply learn to live with their problems."

Cary said, "Well, this time that's *not* the way it's going to be!" She looked intensely at Jacob. "Tell them that I will take her to the clinic the ministry supports, not far from here. I think we passed it, didn't we?" She paused and Jacob nodded. "OK. Have them dress her and we'll go."

He told the family. An older sister brought out a dress to put it on the little one. The dress had a tight-looking neckline and tight sleeves. Cary remembered that the skin on the girl's shoulder was sloughing off already, and she knew that this dress would cause a lot of pain.

"No!" Everyone froze. She turned to Jacob. "Tell them that would hurt. Have them put a loose top on her. She doesn't have to be specially dressed to go see a nurse. They need to understand that."

He explained. They did what Cary told them to do. The wounded girl, her older sister, and Jacob and Cary got in the van and went to the clinic.

When they pulled up under the trees on the edge of the clinic site, people were sitting in the shade. A number were lined up being examined by a nurse. Cary would determine where they should sit and wait for the next nurse to care for them. Cary took the girl's hand and walked towards the nurse. The nurse stopped what she was doing and came over.

"This little one has been burned by boiling water. Her family has no salve or other medicine to help her. I knew you would be able to help, so I brought her here."

The nurse smiled very gently, moved the shirt away from the wounds, and looked a bit startled. "Yes, Madam, this is serious. I will do so right away."

The nurse quickly went to the medicine area and returned with a creamy salve, spreading it gently over the entire area. Then she found some gauze and tape and covered it loosely. She gave the older sister some pain pills and told them to come back the following week so they could reassess the burns.

When they returned to their home, everyone was obviously very pleased that their little one had been helped.

Later Cary realized that she knew no names, nothing. Also, they didn't know her for more than that hour. Cary wondered if, years later, they would think God had dropped an angel into their lives at just the right time. She'd know when she got to heaven.

Unfortunately, Pastors Justin and Jacob hadn't finished the document. Jacob took Cary back to the office. "I'll go back to his house. He will have signed it in a short time and I will bring it to you. I can tell this has been a hard morning for you, seeing how that child was suffering. I think you need to rest."

JOANNE NORTON

CHAPTER FIFTEEN

When Cary walked in the office door, Jill was teary and upset, something that rarely happened.

"Cary, Kevina, the lady we met yesterday at the café, works a few doors down from us. She told me that there are two young kids at the hospital. The boy is about fourteen and the girl is about twelve. The girl is caring for him and he is very ill. They have been living 'rough' for some weeks, staying on the streets, and given absolute minimal care. Kevina wants us to help them, because their business is only helping *young* children. Her story touched me." Jill sat quietly for a few seconds. "What do you think?"

Cary flung her bag onto her desk. Then she took a few minutes to tell Jill what she had walked through at Pastor Justin's. When she finished she said, "We don't have the money for something like that. Our funds are to go through the pastors or other groups. Not directly from us. And after what I walked through, taking that little one to the clinic, I can't make another move in that direction."

Jill looked frustrated, but she didn't say a word. The two of them had a quiet afternoon. They didn't talk much between each other and no one else came into the office. Jill headed back to the compound and Cary stayed for another stretch of time. She felt sad about the kids, and she didn't know what to do.

Cary left the office with her backpack and a pile of extra notebooks in a satchel she had dug from the office. When she reached the corner she saw David with his bike. "David, can you take me? I need help with my books."

"Yes, Madam. Good to help you." He put the backpack and satchel on the front of the bike and Cary sat on the back, side-saddled, fairly comfortable since she had done it more than once now. She was no longer worried about people thinking how funny it was to watch an older-looking white woman on the back of a bike.

While riding past some vendors on the side of the road, she tapped David and asked him to stop. "I want some oranges from this lady." She hopped off the bike, grabbed some shillings out of her backpack, and turned to the woman with the oranges in a black plastic bag at her feet. "Madam, I would like ten of your oranges." When the lady looked at her, Cary realized her words hadn't gotten through.

She called David over. "Will you ask her for ten of the oranges? You work out the cost. I don't have much." David spoke with her and she could tell he was bartering the cost. He finally turned and said, "She will take 1,000 Ush." Cary nodded and handed her the money. The cost was high, but she knew the woman needed every shilling she could earn. Cary also knew that because she was white, people assumed she was rich. She often tried to fight that mentality, but she didn't want to bother this time. She took the bagged-up oranges from the woman and climbed back onto the bike. When David rode past the IDP camp, Cary started tossing the oranges to the people standing near the pathway. They laughed and cheered and jumped to catch the fruit. Cary saw a pregnant lady standing near the path under a tree, and after tapping David to get him to stop, Cary took an orange over to her. The mother broke into a huge smile and gripped Cary's hand tightly. Cary grinned and headed back to the bike.

Everyone waved at her as David started riding the path again. When Cary reached the compound she could hardly believe how happy she was after being so stressed and sad when she left the office. David was obviously very pleased, as he gave her a big smile and wouldn't accept a tip when she paid him for the ride. "I will watch and see if you need a ride, Madam. I like to take you."

Cary went to the room. Jill lay on the bed, a book in her hand. She still had a quiet, withdrawn look on her face. Not angry, just sad.

Cary sat on the end of the bed. "I'm sorry. The Lord reminded me that he's the one calling the shots around here. Not me. The pastors may need funds from the financial source. If someone else needs help for whom we'd need to make an exception to the rules, we can take care of the needs as much as possible. We might not be able to do *too* much, but we can do some. I still have plenty of personal cash. I have been trying to be really careful because I don't know what is ahead. However, God is my financial comptroller. I need to trust *him*, not *me*." Cary tapped Jill's foot. "So, tomorrow we will see if Kevina is available to take one of us to the hospital and check on those kids. OK?"

Jill nodded and smiled. "OK. Thanks, Cary."

After dinner, things quieted down. Many of the African ministry students had gone to other parts of Uganda to stay with family and friends. Some of them from the Congo, Sudan, and Kenya had gone with Ugandan students whose families were willing and able to share their homes. As a consequence, other than a little noise filtering in from the nearby camps, the silence was quite enjoyable.

Cary thought again how thankful she was for Jill and their friendship. She felt blessed as her desire to help others was deepening, and as they settled down for the night, she basked in the rest that could only come from the Holy Spirit.

JOANNE NORTON

CHAPTER SIXTEEN

As soon as they reached the office, Cary did what she had promised. She went to the aid office to find Kevina and tell her they were willing to see how they could help. She was not there, but Cary left a message with one of Kevina's co-workers.

Pastors Joseph, Jacob, John, Job, George, and Justin all came through for a few minutes, long enough to give receipts and receive money for their individual needs. Since Justin didn't have a car or a phone, he usually didn't need much. Today, however, he needed Cary to send a response to Pastor Godfrey, in regards to the document he had received and read the day before.

"Can you please do this for me?"

"I'd be more than happy to do it for you. I am amazed at the people who can email, when so few people here have learned to type. Let's go over to the office."

The busyness of the morning kept her mind occupied. Cary answered emails and spoke with the pastors as they dropped in for finances, receipts, and suggestions. In the process, she had forgotten about Kevina until she looked up and saw her standing at their door.

Kevina smiled. "I am so pleased that you and Jill will see these children. They are hurting so much, and we have been wanting to help them, but the rules in our organization won't let us."

Cary smiled gently. "Jill and I believe the Lord wants us to help, so we will do what we can. I will stay here and you take Jill with you, because her heart is the one that God called. I'll wait."

Jill jumped up, grabbed her purse, and headed for the door. "I'll be back as soon as I can and I'll tell you what it's like."

During the next hour, Cary finished Pastor Justin's email and coordinated her receipts and the cash output. She was beginning to clear the desk when Jill came in, tears flowing.

"Oh, Cary. It's so sad. Boniface is about fourteen and has been in and out of the hospital clinic for nearly six weeks, but wasn't allowed into the hospital ward until a few days ago. He and his sister were dumped in the area by a relative, because Boniface was sick and they couldn't help him. I think the person who dumped them off a *boda* was a brother-in-law in his late teens. Anyhow, as I said, sometimes Boniface would be in the clinic for a quick treatment and the rest of the time they stayed on the street. No money, no food, *nothing*! His sister is Ipullet, which isn't even a real name, but I've been told it means 'little bellybutton'. Well, a few days ago, he finally ended up so ill that they were able to take him into the hospital. The doctors indicated they had wanted to, but because of the crowds of injured people from the invasion, they could only let in someone who was critically ill. He has a fever. In the hospital room there is very little food or water, no pain meds, no blankets. He has only a pair of shorts and a ragged shirt. It's so sad. People in the yard have given some food to Boniface and Ipullet when they've had extra, because they love her. But everyone is *so poor*." Jill started crying again. Cary was amazed, because Jill never had opened up like that. This was one serious situation that God had dropped into their laps.

"What do they need?" Cary asked.

"I'm not sure. Let's dig through the piles of clothes in the back of the room and grab a pair of sweatpants and a warmer shirt for him. When we go shopping we can get a wash basin, soap, and a blanket." Jill sighed heavily. "We need one of the pastors to help us, but I don't know who we can call. Everyone is out with family or church members."

They were digging through the clothes when the door opened and Pastor Joseph came in with his two children. "Hello, Cary and Jill. I want you to meet my—"

Before he had a chance to even finish his sentence, Cary and Jill jumped up and dumped the story on him. He said, "One of you come with me and I will go to the hospital and see them." Cary quickly nodded at Jill, and Jill grabbed her purse. She and Joseph and his children rushed out. Cary sat in the quiet office and prayed that the Lord would open all the right doors at all the right times.

Less than an hour later the two of them walked back into the office. Joseph said, "I dropped my girls off at home, and when we reached the hospital all the pieces came together. The doctors told me that Boniface will have surgery tomorrow. His abdomen is swollen, his pain and temperature are both very high. Jill and I were immediately drawn to Ipullet and her care for her brother and the respect she had from the people around her." He pulled out a shopping list. "We'll go purchase these items."

Jill grabbed the clothes for Boniface. "I want to find some for Ipullet, too." She quickly found a dress and floppy pair of shoes. "When I saw her wearing that 'old lady' dress, I wanted to find something smaller for her. This should look a little better. She doesn't have shoes; I don't think she's ever had any. Her feet look pretty tough."

Cary and Jill gathered everything and headed to Joseph's car. By the time they finished shopping they had filled the car trunk. Charcoal, cooking grill, pans, oil, some beans and grain that Ipullet could use to make some easy-to-swallow food for her brother, bars of both dish soap and body soap, a wash basin, plastic drinking cups, toothpaste and toothbrushes, and blanket. In response to the doctor's request, they also purchased some pain medicine for post-surgery, since the hospital had none. The total came to approximately thirty dollars. Cary and Jill were thrilled that they could use their own money to meet these needs.

As they pulled into the parking area, Ipullet came running out of the hospital to greet them. She immediately stole Cary's heart. Ipullet was obviously very excited to see Jill and Joseph, and when he opened the trunk she started shrieking with delight as he handed her the huge charcoal bundle. Cary mused on how her own kids, grandkids and church kids would never have appreciated something this basic and boring.

When they walked into the hospital, everyone stopped and stared. Joseph said quietly, tears in his voice, "I hate going to the hospitals and walking through the wards. There is so much need and pain."

When Cary saw Boniface, her heart broke and her eyes welled. She turned towards a window and wiped her eyes and cheeks, then went back to Joseph and Jill. There were about thirty men in the room, watching everything from their beds.

Joseph went through the clothes and put a sweatshirt and sweatpants on Boniface. He also showed him the toothbrush and toothpaste, and Ipullet held up the dish soap and body soap, bursting with joy.

Boniface looked and tried to respond, but he had a hard time keeping his eyes open, and his body shivered. When Cary touched him, she was horrified. "Jill, he's so very, very hot. I've never felt heat expanding like this. At first, I thought it was hot here because of the sun and closed windows, but the heat is radiating from him."

Joseph frowned. "I feel it, also. I've been in this room a number of times, but never felt anything this hot. I was nearly crying, too."

A nurse came out of the near room and thanked them for the clothes and the medicine. The hospital had nothing. All she had been able to do was put his bed right near her office windows so she could run out if something serious happened.

When the nurse went away, Joseph offered to take a photo of Boniface, Ipullet, Jill, and Cary. Ipullet held Boniface's hand and pulled him into a sitting position. Cary sat next to Ipullet and could feel the heat emanating from his body even with his sister in between them. Ipullet smiled, but Boniface looked to be in pain. He bent and groaned.

Joseph drew Cary and Jill and Ipullet together, and the four of them held hands as Joseph prayed intensely. "Our dear Father, we love you and we can trust only you to bring healing to Boniface. We know your heart is for us and for him and, no matter what occurs, we trust you. With everything that's happened during these months, and many are in heaven with you now, we know you are the only one who knows the conclusion. However, we love you. Besides Boniface, please touch the other men in this room and the ladies in the room across from us. We love you and we trust you. Bless you, dear Father."

Cary prayed with her eyes open, looking around the ward. She saw the sadness on people's faces. They had obviously become attached to these dear kids, even with their own serious problems.

As they were leaving, the doctor approached. "Thank you for coming and providing the pain medicine and the warm clothes. Our hearts have been turned to these young people, but especially to the girl. She has served her brother in ways none of us have ever seen before. Such love pours from her. We know he is in serious condition, but we are hoping the surgery tomorrow will turn all of this around for them. Thank you again." He nodded to each of them individually.

As they walked out, Cary recognized a nurse named Pauline from the women's area. She grabbed Cary's arm and pulled her into the room. "Look at that lady, Cary. She's the one I told you about who lost her leg."

Cary looked at the young woman, barely out of her teens, lying in her bed and laughing. Cary was stunned. The story went through her mind rapidly. A week earlier Pauline came into the office and sat down, shaking her head. "I worked all night. A woman was brought in whose husband and two boys were killed by the rebels. She was shot in the leg, and the doctors had to amputate it."

Cary had been saddened at such horror, and had assumed the woman would be in her late thirties, with teenaged sons who were fighting the rebels. When Cary saw her in the hospital and realized she was a very young woman, she knew that the boys had been babies, maybe toddlers, and their dad a young man. Cary couldn't conceive how it was possible to have lost a husband, two babies and a leg and *still be smiling*.

"Maybe," Cary said to Pauline, "it's because they understand the tragedies of life in a way I never will. They put their trust in God and move on in life."

With the care and concern of the other patients, with the doctors and nurses, the small amount of supplies that had been given to them, and the way their hearts had been drawn to these children, all Cary could hope for was a continuation of their time together. She decided to email Sam later in the day and see if he would be able to fit Ipullet and Boniface into his orphan ministry. She'd been able to help with their physical needs, but if God had put these two into her life, she didn't want to leave the job half-done.

Joseph drove them to the YWAM complex. As they got out of the car, Cary touched his shoulder. "If any of the pastors have a serious issue come up today, you can come and grab us, but otherwise, it's a blessing to have a few extra hours of rest. We're both heartbroken. Thank you so much for taking us to the pharmacy and the hospital, for letting us provide whatever we could for Boniface and Ipullet. You are very much appreciated."

Jill and Cary linked arms and walked into the office complex.

CHAPTER SEVENTEEN

After they returned from the hospital, Cary and Jill decided to go immediately to the Rescued Children's Camp for more interviews, since their time in Soroti would soon be done. They took a *boda* ride over, closer from town than from the compound the previous weekend. It was hot, but not exceptionally so. For some reason there were fewer kids around. As Jill and Cary stood outside the main building, a woman walked out from the side tent, waving at a few of the teens.

Jill and Cary waited to see if she would come their way. She did. She looked old and very tired. She wore a reddish traditional Ugandan dress and a yellow head covering, and she was very dusty.

Cary smiled at her. "Hello, Madam."

The woman nodded and spoke in easily understood English. "Hello. My name is Modesto."

Cary and Jill introduced themselves.

Jill asked, "Do you know the children who are here? Is that why you came?"

She nodded seriously. "Yes. I know a number of the children. I came to see if my daughter, Betty, had been found. The young men from our village remember seeing her in a rebel camp much farther to the north."

"I'm so sorry," Cary said. "How old is she? When was she captured?"

"She is thirteen. She was captured four months ago. The rebels invaded our village and the people were running away from them. I was at a hospital caring for my oldest daughter while she was giving birth. I returned to the village the next day and was told that the rebels caught Betty as she ran. I have not heard any reports about her since then."

Cary and Jill both reached out to touch Modesto's arm. Modesto said, "God knows where she is. He will take care of her."

"Where are you from?"

"An IDP camp thirty kilometers to the north."

"Really? How did you reach this camp? Did you just come today?" Cary was amazed.

"Yes. I left the camp this morning. I walked six kilometers to the main highway and was able to ride on the back of a large lorry until we reached this town. I have been here for two hours."

Jill asked, "How are you going to reach the camp again?"

Modesto shrugged. "I do not know. My money is finished. I must walk."

Cary and Jill looked at each other. Cary said, "We'd love to give you enough to make it back, but we did not bring very much money with us. We left nearly all our money at the office, except for what we are going to pay for our rides and a couple of other needs."

Jill grabbed Cary and pulled her aside. "We can always give her what we have and then have the riders wait downstairs while we go to the office to get the money for them, and the other stuff can wait."

"Good thinking," Cary said. Then she turned to Modesto. "We will give you the money we have. This will give you enough to ride a lorry and when you are near the camp, maybe someone can give you a *boda* ride there. We don't want you to walk any more than necessary."

Modesto smiled. "Thank you very much. It will help me be home before the day ends."

The rest of that day went normally, although concern for Ipullet and Boniface sat in the back of their minds. Questions of when his surgery would take place, how things would go, when they would hear. As they closed down the office and headed back to the compound, they called Joseph.

"I was told the surgery will begin early this evening. The doctors have been too busy all day to make it happen. I will be checking in as often as is reasonable and will let you know as soon as I can."

With only a few days left before returning to Sam's, Cary felt the tension building in her heart.

CHAPTER EIGHTEEN

Jill and Cary were running a bit late on Friday morning, as they'd unexpectedly had the chance to switch bedrooms. Anne and Allen had left for Jinja for the training session they were running, and Cary and Jill moved into the room. It was larger, with a bathroom and two twin beds. Carrying their items in and rearranging their things took some time. Even though they would only be there for a few days before heading to Kampala, they were excited to have a larger, quieter, more private room.

As they walked across the IDP camp, a car approached, driving across the field instead of the road. It was Joseph. They rushed to him, and as they climbed in the car, they asked, "What happened? How is Boniface?"

Joseph's face was somber. "This is our challenge for today. He died."

The three of them sat in the car and cried together. Cary called Sue. "So sorry to wake you, honey. But I needed to tell you. The boy died."

Sue nearly hugged her through the phone. "Oh, no." She paused, and then said quietly and gently, "I wish I could be there with you, Mom." Cary cried quietly. "Is there anything I can do?"

Cary said, "Only pray. I don't know what I will have to do today to help. So much could happen. Mostly, I want to do whatever is necessary to keep Ipullet and take her to Sam."

"Well, call when you can. Anytime. We miss you, and you undoubtedly are appreciated there."

"Thank you, hon. Today's going to be a rough one. Love you, dear. Bye for now."

Cary closed her phone. Joseph and Jill had been conversing quietly while she and Sue were talking. Cary hoped they had made some decisions about the day.

Jill said, "Cary, Joseph and Jacob will take you to buy the coffin and burial cloths. I will stay at the hospital with Pauline and watch as the nurses and others make any of the family connections that we don't know of. Maybe someone will walk in when the news goes out. It is amazing how quickly this news spreads." Joseph nodded.

Cary asked, "Where will the money come from and how much will it cost? In all the time I've been in Uganda, even with friends who have attended several burials in only one week, I've never been in the right place at the right time. I don't know anything about it."

"For us, this will cost a great deal and we have very little. Can you take the money from the ministry fund? We can talk to the administrators, but they won't be available during this stretch of time and you will be gone for that time."

Cary thought about it for only a few seconds. "Yes, Joseph, we will. If they don't like the decision, then Jill and I will do what we can to cover that cost from our personal accounts." Jill nodded. Cary continued. "We must keep all the receipts though, very carefully, especially since we can't discuss this with any of the leadership first."

A while later, Pauline, who had worked the night shift at the hospital, arrived to make sure all the proper details were in place. She knew the "Western ladies" wouldn't notice if they were being cheated in terms of costs. Cary and Jill often wondered when Pauline ever slept, between the clinic ministry, the hospital job, and raising four teenaged girls.

Cary headed out with Joseph and Jacob to make the necessary purchases. It took a couple of hours. Cary didn't have to do much except dig through the purse and give the money. She saw Jacob arguing with the coffin seller, and could tell that he was very angry, which she had never seen before. When he climbed back into the van, after he and Joseph had managed to slide the coffin in the back, he was still pretty upset. He finally said, "That young boy died. We needed a coffin. And this man wanted to charge *extra*, because he saw you sitting here and he thought that if a white woman was in the van we could pay him much more money. I talked him out of that, but I wanted to, as you folks sometimes say, punch his lights out." He almost smiled and nodded tensely. "I didn't."

Cary grinned at him. "I'm glad you didn't, but I agree that it is so difficult when this becomes the norm—seeing people from other countries and assuming they are rich."

As they arrived at the hospital to pick up Ipullet and Jill and to put Boniface's body into the coffin, they saw some people just standing around. Many of them spoke about how special Ipullet and Boniface were.

They passed a doctor on their way inside, and he stopped them, teary. "The boy had an enlarged spleen and was anemic. There was nothing we could do to save him. I *never* cry over a patient. I never have. But the girl…" He shook his head. "If I could keep her in my home, I would take her." As he walked away he mumbled, "But I can't."

Joseph and Jacob looked at each other and sighed. The men and Cary walked into the hospital and found Jill, Pauline, and Ipullet sitting on a bench inside a small reception area. Pauline immediately stood and headed towards them.

"We were told that no one will be available to wrap Boniface's body in the burial cloths. You must do it."

Cary was horrified that these pastors would be placed in that position, but they just looked at her and shrugged their shoulders. Joseph said, "We have had to do this before. It is not pleasant, but there are so many deaths around us that the preparations must be done by whoever is available. We will take the coffin from the van and meet you there when we're finished."

A short time later, Joseph and Jacob came outside with the coffin and put it in the van. As they stuffed it between a seat and the side door, it tipped. Cary gasped, convinced that Boniface's body had slipped to one side and would push the top off.

Suddenly a group of people ran onto the property, wailing and crying. They claimed to be Boniface's relatives. It almost became a riot. The people on the hospital grounds who had been caring for the children out of their own small belongings and who had watched the children struggle and the boy suffer, were ready to kill the relatives. Cary and Jill were furious, too. But soon the story came out and eventually everyone settled down.

A sister of Boniface's father, although he was not Ipullet's dad, calmed everyone and told their side. She said, "Our half-sister had been told a number of times by her 'husband', a young man who had dumped the two kids off from his bike a few weeks ago, that Boniface was doing better. This morning, she finally came to see him and was told he had died. And she ran to our home, near here, screaming in grief over the death of her nephew. We did not know Boniface was there, and in fact had not known Ipullet at all, since she had a different father. The mother had isolated herself from the Soroti family and died several months ago."

What created most of the confusion was that, for some reason, the nineteen-year old half-sister had not let either side of the family know about the presence of the other one. Since the other family only lived a few blocks away, they could have been there to help Ipullet and provide financial aid and food and other needs. As soon as they were told about the death, they rushed to the hospital and into the hospital yard.

After listening, Cary thought, "This sounds like something straight out of a movie. How strange!"

CHAPTER NINETEEN

The next day Cary sent an email to Pastor Max to tell him all the rest of the events of that day.

=============

Dear Pastor,

My dear patient pastor, this is long and detailed. But you need to see how things went and how strangely the day progressed after the death. The hospital stories will be sent separately, but I know this will really get your attention. Since my dear hubby and I had heard much about this country and had gone around a bit, I realize how it sometimes feels that all you do here is drive around in circles.

Here goes.

It was nearly noon when all of this came together and we had to find a burial spot, since, as you know, burials here are nearly always done on the same day as the death. However, their mother, who had died just a few months earlier, was buried in what had become a particularly dangerous rebel area, and going there might have left us open to attack. The relatives contacted another member of the family who was some sort of doctor and had some land out in the bush—way out in the bush—and he said they could bury the boy out there. During all this decision-making we all were crammed into the car and van, and we were going around in circles. Jill, Pauline, Ipullet, and I were in a very small, low-to-the-ground car with Joseph. BTW, Jill and I insisted that Ipullet not be in the van, since the coffin lid was so iffy. We didn't want her to see her brother that way. So Jacob drove the van full of the relatives and the coffin, which was still crammed in at an angle. We finally all headed out to the burial area. Well, we went round and round, this road and that, following bicycle trails, driving through elephant grass and across muddy stretches that could well have buried our car. The pastors had cell phones, but there was no connection out there and they lost each other; we sure didn't know where we'd end up. At one point, we had to get out of our car to lighten it so Joseph could get it through a mud hole. The villagers and farmers in the area were given quite a show. Seeing people come through for a burial wouldn't be a shock, but two white women as part of the group? I'll bet that was a real news-maker in the area!

Eventually we connected. The property and its surrounding land were so impoverished. It was heartbreaking to look at it. A few locals had shown up to help dig the grave. However, some time after they had begun, they realized the ground was too hard, so they had to switch to a different part of the yard. They took turns with a pick and shovel and finally reached a reasonable burial depth.

Here's another piece of information we hadn't known. After the burial, the ground is covered with concrete. This keeps animals from digging in and eating the body. Or people breaking in and stealing the coffin for someone else! When Joseph put a few bags of concrete in the van when we were getting the coffin, I didn't understand, but I didn't ask about it. I trusted that, since it was my money, they wouldn't be buying anything unnecessary.

In the meantime, several other women and children came to the burial site, wailing. Turns out they didn't know anyone, but it is a local custom. I took lots of photos: a young goat eating corn cobs and looking around to see if anyone was going to catch him doing it, like any other kid; a little naked boy hanging out by a scrubby tree with a swollen belly that was probably worm-filled; the people digging the grave; Ipullet and her family sitting on a blanket on the ground and sharing together; and, finally, the best one, of Ipullet holding her little baby niece she hadn't seen during her weeks at the hospital. She obviously loved her. Ipullet had a great deal of care and love in her heart towards anyone and everyone who came into her life. Although she was grieving the death of her brother, she was so outgoing towards others that she hardly focused on the reason we were all there.

Through the pastors, all were blessed. They shared a short, very nice service. Even though Joseph is Baptist and Jacob is Anglican, they worked together very faithfully. This was an obvious opportunity to show unity, and they did a beautiful job of it.

Seeing this really blessed me. My husband and I worked as hard as we could to break down those irrational, unnecessary doctrines or traditions that kept people apart. It was so good to see them doing the same thing.

Another blessing: After the burial, when back in Soroti, a local authority gave us permission to take Ipullet back to Sam and the Sanyu Home. That in itself was short of a miracle. After the burial service we returned to Soroti, and we left Ipullet with Pauline, so Ipullet could spend time with her teenage girls. We will take her with us in a few days.

I hope this will make you as happy as it did me. Jill and I were able to make good connections with all of Ipullet's family who had rushed to the hospital. They also only live about two blocks from our office. Her grandfather was not able to come as he has trouble walking, so we will be going to meet him on Monday. I think I told you before, but Joseph will be taking us to Kampala and Sam will pick us up there. Whenever we head out, things will change.

I'll be calling you soon, I hope—if the signal is working. That's always the catch.

BTW, I forgot to tell you. You'd laugh! Another day I was in a village for a short visit with one of the pastors and the only place for any signal at all was at the round-about drive area on the entrance of the village and against a metal village entrance sign. I needed to call Sam, and I had to lean against the metal sign, and hold the phone up against it, and couldn't even shift my arm because the signal would drop. Can you imagine how insane that looked? And when a bicyclist or car came through and saw me leaning my head on the metal, I'm sure it looked hilarious. Believe me, I kept that call very, very short!

You are much appreciated and missed, and please spread this info around to my family and the churches.

Cary

JOANNE NORTON

CHAPTER TWENTY

Cary picked up her phone and called her son, Mike. It was nearly midnight on Sunday where he was, about 9:00 Monday morning in Soroti. Hearing his voice, she burst into tears.

"What's wrong, Mom?"

"Somewhere I lost about one-and-a-half million shillings. Maybe more. I have looked through *every*thing and checked *every*where and the money is gone! What am I going to do?"

"Mom, that doesn't make any sense. You are a very careful person."

"I know. Jill keeps the 'millions' in her bag, and I keep the 'thousands' in mine. It seems impossible that some could be gone from both, but it's happened."

"Did you both have your purses with you all the time?"

"I didn't *always* have mine, but she always *did* have hers. Or we locked them in the office very carefully. Even if someone could have done it then, we would have figured it out quickly, because every day we did an accounting to make sure our figures were correct. With everything that happened on Friday, all I can think is that when I was in the van giving money for the burial materials, some money could have fallen out of my purse or someone could have quietly stolen it. That happens so often around here. But it wouldn't have been the million. I spent a couple hundred thousand for the cloth, coffin, and the concrete that was placed over the grave. I didn't go much over that. And Jill never let her bag out of sight."

"Who do you have to tell about this?"

"Oh, Mike, please tell Pastor Max, because he'll call the FAITH ministry leaders from the UK and US and Uganda that were putting this ministry in place. They provided the funding and I have to tell them and try to convince them that I wasn't being foolish or pocketing it for myself. If they fuss about it, I have to give them about seven hundred and fifty dollars to cover this, but I can't afford it. I know that…" She began crying again.

Mike stayed on the phone quietly and let her calm down. "Mom, God is bigger. You say that all the time. Don't let this break your heart. Money is money, and relationships are much more important. We'll trust God to work this out. I know you have folks over there praying for you. And you have many people over here who are supporting you in prayer. I'll call Pastor Max and he'll email them right away. I'll call Sue and Luke and a few others. Keep me posted, call when you can. I know that once you reach Sam's, the chances for a connection are a lot slimmer."

"I don't know what I'd do without you, son. My heart is calmer already."

"We'll trust the Lord. That's all we can do."

"That's right."

They said goodbye at the same time.

CHAPTER TWENTY-ONE

Cary and Jill began to load their clothes, books, and piles of other things into their bags. They needed to leave Soroti in a couple hours to be in Kampala as close to noon as possible. Joseph would take them and drop them off at an eating area downtown and Sam would pick them up. Cary, who rarely was awake at six in the morning, jumped out of bed and started tossing things together. Jill was up soon after, having packed the night before. They both wrote nice notes to Allen and Anne, thankful they'd been able to stay in this room.

At about eight, Cary called Joseph. "I'm on the way," he said. "I have to drop by my church for a few minutes and talk to someone, because I'll be gone for the day. They need to be watching what can happen with those who are staying in our yards. I'll be there in about half an hour."

Cary turned to Jill. "Let's go to the dining area and see if there's anything to eat."

Jill grinned. "Coffee is all that counts with me, as you know. But if there's food, I'll take some."

They grabbed some bread, Jill got her coffee, and Cary ran back to their room to look for something to drink. She dug under the beds and found some water bottles. She grabbed all ten and took them to the eating area, where she found a box with which to carry them. She would drink one here and take the rest along for the trip.

A car entered the compound and honked. It was Joseph. They took what they could, and then Cary went to the kitchen and asked one of the teens to carry the rest of their bags. One of the boys rushed out to do it. He thanked them for being there and helping so many for these weeks. Cary gave him a little hug and thanked him for his helpfulness.

Joseph looked at his small car. "I hope everything will fit in here when we pick up Ipullet and put her things in, too."

Jill said, "I doubt she'll have much. She has the clothes she was wearing when we met her—unless they've been thrown away—and the one dress we gave her. Pauline might have given her something. So, I don't think her stuff will take up much space."

Cary laughed. "Once when I was with my friends, Tim and *another* Jill," she winked at Jill, "we went together to southwestern Uganda, not far from Mbarara. That car was *very* full. It was them and their three kids, me, a pastor friend named Isaac, and another lady and her daughter, plus piles of bags. The car was so packed we could hardly move or breathe. This one we're in now is much easier, believe me."

Right then they pulled up downtown, onto a Soroti side-street, and honked. Pauline came out of her small home with Ipullet who carried a small bag. Pauline gave Ipullet a hug. Joseph smiled and let her into the car. Cary was in the front, and Ipullet was with Jill in the back. But only Ipullet and Joseph could speak in the same language. All Cary and Jill could do was hold her hands and encourage her with smiles.

About four hours later they entered Kampala, after having eaten lunch in the Jinja area. Joseph dropped them and their bags off at a downtown restaurant area. "I'm sorry I can't stay with you longer. I have to get on the way northwest to see a group at Fort Portal." He walked to the car and opened the door, then suddenly closed the door and returned to Cary and Jill.

"You dear ladies, thank you so much for what you have done for all of us. I look forward to your return when you have taken Ipullet where she can stay and see some of your own dear friends. I will be back in Soroti in a few days and can hardly wait to see you." He gave a gentle hug to all three of them. They smiled at him, and Cary and Jill expressed their appreciation for all he had done for them.

He left with a honk and a wave.

Jill said, "OK, Cary. Now how do we know what Ipullet needs? We don't know her words."

Cary shrugged. "If we get into a large group of people, there will be someone that will be able to interpret for us."

"Where do you want us to go for that?"

"Well, we ate in Jinja, so let's go to the FAITH place and I'll call Sam and tell him where to pick us up."

"Good idea, Cary. It's only a few blocks from here. Where can we keep the bags?"

"Well, not far down the street is Nakasaro, with the main vegetables and fruits and other good things. I remember a man there helped me many times, even when I was doing something thoroughly dumb. So, I'll run down there and grab him if I can."

Jill and Ipullet sat together right by the street, holding onto their bags. Cary came back in a few minutes, and introduced her friend. "This is another Sam. I met him about ten years ago when we first were shopping there. A missionary from Washington state introduced me to him. Sam said he'd keep these bags behind the boxes in his vegetable stall. I told him we'll be getting them in an about an hour. Oh, and one of his co-workers came and the two of them will carry these things."

As they took the bags, Cary and Jill both smiled and thanked them. Then they turned around and went up the street to the FAITH office. Although Cary had spoken to the people who worked there, she had never been inside.

When they walked in the door, the secretary, Harriet, jumped up. "Oh, Jill, it's wonderful to see you. I know you were here a few weeks ago, and you were sent to Soroti, but you weren't given any job to do up there. We expected you would walk around until your partner arrived." She smiled. "And you must be Cary. We saw a photo of you, and we've spoken on the phone. Now I finally get to meet you. What a blessing to have the two of you walk in now!"

All three of them laughed. They also introduced Ipullet, and Harriet could talk to her. Cary and Jill didn't understand a word, but Harriet and Ipullet seemed to be having a very friendly conversation. Cary told Harriet they would explain her story more clearly later.

Harriet suddenly said to Jill, "I've tried to call you and tell you the next plan. I haven't been able to reach you."

Jill shrugged her shoulders. "Sorry. Sometimes the phones don't connect well enough, as you know."

"What I needed to tell you is that you are not going back to Soroti."

Jill said, "*What?*" Cary looked horrified.

Harriet said. "Sorry, Jill. And you too, Cary. Jill, you need to go back to England to the FAITH location there, as they need someone to speak at different churches and share about this ministry. They know you'd be wonderful."

"When do I need to leave? Can I stay for a while?"

"No. In fact, now that you've shown up, we'll take you to Entebbe and keep you at a hotel tonight and send you off tomorrow."

As Cary and Jill were processing this information, suddenly Ipullet said to Harriet that she needed to squat someplace so she wouldn't be wetting. Harriet pointed to a door, and Ipullet looked inside, but she obviously didn't know what to do. Cary, who needed to use the toilet, realized that for the first time in her life she needed to show someone how to use a toilet. So Cary pulled down her panties, sat on the toilet, did her peeing, wiped herself, stood up, and flushed the toilet, with Ipullet standing right inside the door to see what Cary was doing. Ipullet's eyes got very big. Cary pointed at the toilet and touched everything that Ipullet needed to do, and Cary stepped out so she could do this privately. A couple minutes later, when Ipullet flushed, she laughed and screamed and when she ran out the door, she still was laughing. However, she was dry.

Cary said to Jill and Harriet, "I've taught a lot of things and a lot of people, but I have never shown a kid how to sit on a toilet and how to do the wiping and the flushing. How embarrassing is that? But it looks like she was able to do it. And very happy that you had a bowl to wash our hands in, too."

Harriet said, "Thanks. I would have done this, since I had her language, but I appreciate your willingness. You are a real blessing."

Jill asked, "Do I need to head down the street to get my bags?"

Harriet said, "No. You tell us where they are, and we'll have one of our workers pick it up."

"No, Harriet," Cary said. "I need to go down, too, because those protectors who are keeping them won't give them away. I'll be glad if someone comes with me. Actually, I'll grab Ipullet's hand and take her. She'll see a new part of the world. This is quite amazing to her."

"OK. Jill needs to stay here and talk to me and Peter. He'll be coming in the door in a couple minutes. He went to the post office, and that does take a while, as you probably know."

Cary and Jill both rolled their eyes and nodded. The lines in post office were a sure way to kill time.

Cary patted Ipullet and held her hand. She and Ipullet, along with the young guy from the office went down the street to get their bags.

"Samuel, thank you so much for keeping these here. If one of you can come, the four of us can carry these to the FAITH room."

119

Samuel smiled. He gave bags to the three of them and took a few himself, and they quickly took everything to FAITH. Everyone smiled at Samuel and thanked him. Cary held his hand and smiled. "It's been too long since I've seen you. You sure were a treat from '94 to '96 when we came in here last. Thank you so much."

"You are welcome. You have been a blessing for us, too."

When he left, Cary turned to Jill. "So, when are you leaving?"

She said, "In about an hour I'll be taken to Entebbe. Tomorrow morning I'll be at the airport and home in England about noon, local time."

"So how do we stay in touch? When I have a serious situation in Soroti can I call you?"

"Yes. You can call any time. I might be able to pray for you, or encourage you, or message you with info. We're a little different in our way of viewing things, especially the situation that opened up with Boniface, but we entered that strongly. I appreciate you. I'll miss you. And by the way, when you are coming through England, I'll try to meet you at the airport and spend a few hours with you, because it's usually at least a six-hour layover."

Cary smiled and pulled Jill in for a hug, both of them laughing and crying.

An hour later, Sam arrived at the FAITH office and was even able to park nearby. As he climbed out of his car, Jill was leaving in the office car, and Cary stood by and waved at her. Cary turned and saw him, and pointed them out to each other. Cary knew those two would have been great co-workers.

CHAPTER TWENTY-TWO

One of the immediate blessings was that Sam could understand Ipullet, even though they spoke different tribal languages. The Teso language is Nilotic, while Sam's tribal language was one of the Bantu languages. While some African countries might have only one native language, Uganda has several, with many dialects, and Sam, like many Ugandans, had at least a basic grasp of multiple languages.

When Sam finished speaking with Ipullet, he said, "I really want to keep this girl with us! She has a real heart for people, and cares for them. Even though her brother died, she is facing the future. She loved him and said goodbye, even though he died in the surgical room. I think Adhe would really want her, too."

When Sam finished talking, Cary's phone rang. It was Jill. "Hey, Cary. I had a thought. Ipullet's name needs to be changed from 'little belly button'. I was thinking of Sanyu. What do you think?"

"Good idea, but Sam's ministry title is 'Sanyu'. I don't know if he'll feel that would conflict. I'll bring it up to him and Adhe later today. Oh, and one of the funny things has been to watch Ipullet see the business towers, the streets, the stop lights, the large churches. When she's looking around and about her eyes are huge and her breathing is heavy. She's obviously in a whole different world. When we turn off the main highway area, she'll feel very much at home. It all looks similar to the village area for her. She'll relax a bit, I think. Anyhow, I'll tell them the name idea, and see what happens and call you. Where are you?"

Jill said, "Oh, I'll be in Entebbe in about an hour. The hotel is right by Lake Vic, so, if I have a room to look out that direction, I'll be very happy. That lake and the Nile always make me smile."

"Me, too. I hope you have a great night, and a great flight. I'll bug you when I can."

When Cary put her phone aside, she told Sam. "Jill called because she had thought of a name for Ipullet that would be much nicer. She likes Sanyu, and you probably heard me tell her that it might not work, because of your ministry title. I told her Adhe might have an idea, too."

Sam said, "Yes. We'll see. I definitely agree that her name should be changed. Now, Mom, I have to concentrate on the driving. There are so many holes in the road now, and so many goats and cows out loose, that I have to be especially careful. You hold her hand and smile. That's all that counts. We'll be home in an hour or so."

"You got it, kid. I appreciate what you're doing and where we're going. I think Ipullet will be happy, too."

While sitting in the back seat with her, holding her hand, they both fell asleep.

CHAPTER TWENTY-THREE

When they were close to Sam's house, he woke them.

"What a treat to be here with you, Sam. And what joy it will be for Ipullet to meet Adhe and Stella. I can hardly wait!"

Sam smiled. "When we get here, I'll let Adhe change her name. Ipullet is a funny name, but not very nice. I'm sure she'll pick something very good."

Sam pulled into the driveway, honking. Adhe ran out, with Stella holding her hand, and they both hugged Sam and Cary. Then Sam took Ipullet from the back seat, and held her hand and took her to Adhe. Adhe and Stella smiled, and both of them reached out to touch her.

"I am very happy to meet you." Adhe spoke in English, and Sam translated to Teso. Ipullet smiled bashfully.

They went into the house, and Adhe told Ipullet that she would sleep in Stella's room. Ipullet was happily surprised when Adhe gave her a pretty nightgown and told her what it was for. She washed her feet and brushed her teeth, and then both girls went to bed.

The adults sat in the living room and talked about the name change. Adhe smiled. "I have already decided to name her Rebecca. It is one of my favorite names and giving it to her will be perfect."

Cary returned the smile. "Thank you so much! That's wonderful." After pausing a moment, she said "My dear friend, Jill, who was with me in Soroti and was instrumental in bringing Rebecca to us, came up with 'Sanyu'. I told her that was the name of your ministry home, so it might not work."

Adhe smiled. "That is fine. She is now Rebecca Sanyu. A beautiful name."

"Yes. Thank you. Well, I need to head to my room. This has been a very busy and difficult day. I miss Jill very much already. I'll be phoning her often, I'm sure, but seeing her would be nicer. I wish you could have met her, Adhe."

"Yes. I've heard much about her. If I'm ever in England, I'll certainly try to connect with her. Or if she returns to Uganda, I'll rush around to find her. She sounds wonderful."

"Hope you two sleep well. I'll see you in the morning." She hugged both of them tightly. "I missed you two so much. I wish I could always stay with you, but eventually I need to head out to Soroti and then home. Oh, well."

Cary went to her room. She pulled the mosquito netting aside, crawled into the bed, and made sure that the net was tucked under her mattress. In spite of it being warm inside the netting, she went to sleep and slept right through the night.

When Cary walked into the house the next morning, Rebecca and Stella were eating breakfast. There was a platter of sliced bananas, mangos, and pineapples on the table. Adhe got up to prepare some chai tea for Cary.

"Hi, Grandma," Stella said. She jumped off her chair and ran to her. Cary picked her up and kissed her cheek. When she put her down, Rebecca came to her and smiled. She felt Cary's hair and looked confused. Then, surprisingly, she said, "You chicken feathers."

Cary felt her hair and laughed. She had forgotten to comb it, so it was sticking up, and with all the dust from traveling, it was quite stiff.

"Adhe, how did she come up with English words? I've never heard her say anything in English!"

"Well, Mum, Sam found out early this morning that she does know some English and other languages from the little bit she was in school. She's a smart girl."

Cary smiled. "Has Rebecca adjusted to her new name?"

"Yes, she has! She likes both of the names. I'm very grateful that Jill suggested 'Sanyu'!"

During the morning, Cary and Adhe walked with Rebecca to a nearby home where several girls lived. Rebecca wore the same dress, because Adhe didn't have clothes for her. After proper greetings were exchanged, they went into the house. The mother and girls were excited to give Rebecca some clothes, and she kept laughing as she tried on shirts, skirts and shoes. At the end of their visit, they had a nice pile of clothes for Rebecca.

When Sam arrived, Rebecca ran out and grabbed his hand and pulled him inside. She counted the clothes spread out in the living room, laughing as she counted from one to thirteen. Sam couldn't help but laugh at her excitement, and he held her hand and told her that she looked very pretty in her new clothes. Her shirt was bright red with a colorful, flowered skirt. Cary and Adhe smiled and laughed with them. Stella jumped up and down and laughed, too.

Later, as Cary walked to her room when it was dark and hot, she prayed, rejoicing. "Thank you, dear Lord, because this day was filled with joy, with friendship, with significant gifts from you. What a blessing today has been. Again, thank you!"

She got to her door and had to lower her arms to get inside, as she'd raised them to the sky in worship.

JOANNE NORTON

CHAPTER TWENTY-FOUR

"Mom!... Mom!" Cary heard Sam shouting and knocking on her door. She called out to him and he stopped making noise. She jumped out of bed, wrapped a shawl around her, and opened the door.

"What's going on? Is something wrong?"

"I got a call from one of my sisters. She is visiting my mother and says she's very, very sick. She's in our home village in the central-western area. I go out once in a while, and my sisters and brothers call me when they visit. I'm the youngest, but sometimes the busiest." Normally very calm, Cary had never seen him look stressed before.

"So what are you going to do? Are we going? If so, when?"

"I'll take Adhe and the girls there. I'll have to drop you off in Kampala, because you need to return to Soroti soon. You've been with us almost a week now, and that's been a blessing for us."

"It's been a blessing to me, too. Before heading to Soroti, I wanted to spend a night or two in a hotel in Kampala. After you drop me off, I'll hang out, and then get on a bus. I've been afraid to do that, but God will protect me, I'm sure. How soon do you want to leave?"

"I would like to leave in about an hour. I'm sorry that you have to pack your bags so quickly."

"That's OK, Sam. I haven't unloaded much of it, so it won't take long. I'll get dressed and be ready by then. Spending time riding with the four of you will be nice."

They left on time, and they waved goodbye to the three ladies who were staying to take care of the house and yard.

Cary enjoyed the drive, its laughter and chatter, and Adhe translated some of Rebecca's conversation. Cary reveled in the green hills and trees, as there were so few trees and so little green in Soroti. "I've loved trees since I was a child, and I used to climb quite high in them. I'd sit on the branches and read my books, and none of my family would even think of me for a little while. I also climbed up them very high to eat the cherries and grab some apples. I quit when I was about twelve years old, because I'd started to fall a bit and I got scared. But I still *love* seeing and touching trees."

Cary smiled as they entered Kampala. "It's been a while now since I've been here. And I'm so excited to stay here. I will trust you to take me to a good hotel—you pick."

Sam chuckled. "The hotel is where you and Dad and your Ugandan sister, Trudy, ate that one time. You sure loved the restrooms compared to anything you'd seen in Kenya and Uganda by then."

"Oh, the Sheraton. On that first trip, James and I were able to get to this hotel a few times for one reason or another. Going into the restrooms was one of my favorite things to do. So clean, and with nice soap and water and nice odors. Homes or churches on that trip were often pretty smelly."

"Yes, you guessed correctly—that's where I'm dropping you off. You'll have taxis or *bodas* to take you wherever you want to go. Not too expensive."

"OK." She paused. "Sheraton Hotel is also in other countries, including ours where it began many years ago. I was shocked when I saw it here in '91. I've heard that there are hundreds of these hotels. My heavens!"

"We're only a couple minutes away. We'll all get out and give you a hug."

She smiled sadly. "I'd like that. How about I pray now?"

Adhe said, "Oh! Thank you, Mum!"

They spread their hands around, and she touched Sam's shoulder. "Dear Father, please protect Sam as he's driving in a dangerous area where the roads are not solid. Protect this family as they head to another part of the nation. Please give Sam and Adhe an opportunity to pray over his mother and, if needed, to know where to take her to a doctor. When the family sees Stella, please give them a love for her. When they meet Rebecca and find out she is from the Soroti area which is full of pain and suffering, please let them encourage her. Thank you, Lord, for Sam and Adhe bringing me down and how they've encouraged me and shown appreciation for my Soroti God-job from you. Thank you, Lord, and bless you."

As soon as they pulled into the hotel driveway, Cary got out. Adhe immediately came out and said, "I'll miss you so much, Mum. You are a blessing to me." She kissed her on the cheek. Cary grabbed her hand and kissed it as she was switching to the front seat. When the girls jumped out to hug her goodbye, Cary was filled with joy. When she walked to the driver side of the car, Sam stepped out and gave her a big, strong hug. They kissed cheeks, then he jumped in and headed out the driveway. They all waved at her, and she smiled and waved until the car had disappeared.

Cary went into the hotel and checked in, and she was soon in a room five floors up. She put the bags by the window and looked out at the tall birds on the nearby trees. She loved seeing them and stood in the window for a few minutes and waved at them. Some of them flew away. Some of them looked like they were smiling.

She went downstairs and went outside and asked the clerk to order a motorcycle to take her to the National Theatre area. She wanted to walk through those shops and find something Ugandan that she could bring home. She had been there many times in the previous years.

The motorcycle soon arrived. She could wear jeans and sit normally since she was in Kampala, and the ride would be safer and more comfortable.

Soon the motorcycle dropped her off at the shopping area. She walked around, enjoying looking at the art, crafts, clothes, and jewelry.

"Thank you so much, Madam, for these wonderful earrings," Cary said as she took a pair that had been made from cattle's horns and dyed purple. "These will make me smile every time I wear them." She paid and kept exploring. She wanted a dress, but they were too expensive.

She walked through a few more shops, avoiding the ones that sold idols—gods that had been worshiped for hundreds of years in various tribes. The shop where she found the jewelry was Christian. Then she found another Christian shop that had clothes, including dresses, and she soon found one that perfectly matched her earrings. Now she had plenty of purple.

Cary got a ride back to the hotel and ate dinner, then rested. Knowing she would be heading to Soroti the next day on a bus, she went to bed early. As she settled in and pulled the blankets over her, she rejoiced that she didn't need mosquito nets.

"Thank you, Father. Today was filled with blessings, from leaving Sam's and coming to Kampala. This hotel, the shopping, and that wonderful dinner have all been a treat! Give me strength tomorrow as I go to Soroti, and may I be an encouragement and help to others. Again, thank you, and bless you. I love you. Amen."

She went to sleep immediately. It was unusually quiet that night for a hotel in the city, and she slept straight through.

CHAPTER TWENTY-FIVE

Cary got on the bus and grabbed a window seat. She knew she'd have to be careful when the bus went through towns. Years earlier she was in a taxi going through Kampala, and it was stopped at a stoplight when a boy reached through the window and tore her watch off her wrist. It had been her favorite watch. She'd been reading her French teaching book then, not paying enough attention to the outside. Now when she sat down by the window, she did not put her arm on the open portion. The only book she kept with her was her Bible. She needed to focus on the Lord on her way to Soroti. She made sure she didn't have anything on her wrist, so she could pay attention but not worry.

Surprisingly, there were few people on board at the start of the journey. As they went further through Kampala, then stopped in Jinja, Mbale, and other side towns, they might pick at least another twenty people. She settled in and watched the scenery through Kampala, then read the Psalms.

In Mbale a few people boarded but she was still sitting alone. A short time later, she glanced at the man who had been sitting behind her since she had gotten on the bus. She hadn't talked to anyone the whole time, even though she smiled at people. Now she turned to him.

"Hello. You've been on this bus as long as I have. Where are you going?"

"I am going to Soroti. I was in the Entebbe and Kampala area for a few weeks and now I will be working in Soroti again."

"Oh. What job do you have? I've seen so many in the Soroti area. Some of the work is amazing."

"I am a sergeant in our national army. I'm based there and have been for six years, before this invasion occurred. I consider this very important. I don't want to stay anywhere else."

She smiled and nodded. She had already met several of the Soroti-based military men. They were there, of course, to fight Kony and the LRA, and to keep order in the camps, but they also worked with the youth that had been abducted as young children and used as slaves, some of whom had been forced to kill others. One soldier cried when he came into her office, because he was a pastoral youth teacher and saw so many heading into such danger, both spiritually and physically. He asked her to lay hands on him and pray. He hadn't stopped crying, but was thankful for the prayer and encouragement. Knowing these things, Cary sure had a heart for the military members.

He asked, "Why are you in Soroti?"

"I'm supporting the local pastors as they help the thousands of people running from the LRA. I have a heart for the spiritual warfare groups in Kampala that come up to pray in the northwest portion where Joseph Kony is from."

He smiled. "I'll tell you what I did. A few months ago, some of the ministry people came up to pray over a stream that has been poisonous for hundreds of years. I am a sergeant, as I told you, and we took about twenty men to protect those people. We watched very carefully. As they prayed and praised God, the stream became clear. They drank the water and gave it to the villagers who were with them. We had it, too. I've never seen anything like that in twenty years in the army."

Cary grinned. "Yes! I know the man who is the main leader for spiritual warfare. He is a dentist in Kampala, and he worked on my teeth and my tongue when I was living in the Kampala area several years ago. Actually, last night, when I went downstairs to get dinner in the Sheraton Hotel, he and his wife were walking out of the dining area as I was walking in. We recognized each other after all these years, and it was a blessing to see them. He grabbed my hands and prayed over me for my time in Soroti. Somehow he had heard about that from others in Uganda. What a blessing! And now to know that he brought the people up to minister in this way, I'd have jumped up and down when I saw him. Oh, well. I always say that I'm looking forward to seeing friends in heaven."

The man smiled, too. "It was good to see them and to be there. I have never seen anything quite like that and I am now a different kind of Christian. Oh, and Joseph Kony's mother came to be with them as soon as the stream was repaired. She told them that she wanted to be with Jesus and to be away from her son. He had murdered many in that area."

Cary nodded. "I have heard about his family turning to the Lord. I've also talked with some of the abducted and abused children. They have prayed for him and his helpers, because they want them to be free. This is a difficult thing for your nation. Very sad."

She looked out the windows and saw that they were nearing Soroti. As they'd talked, Cary had not written his name or contact details down. She knew she wouldn't have much time when she got to Soroti, as she had agreed a time and place with Jacob for him to pick her up, so she started scrounging for pen and paper.

A minute later the bus stopped in another entry portion of the town. He smiled and nodded at her as he got off the bus. She hadn't been fast enough.

When the bus stopped at the main location, she got off, and her bags were taken from the roof. Five minutes later Jacob pulled into the parking area near her, called her name, and jumped out of his car to get her things.

He laid his hand on her shoulder and squeezed. "It is a blessing to see you again, Aunt Cary. I hoped Jill would be with you, but I have heard that she is in England now. With the needs we have up here, you have been a blessing. Joseph, George, Job, Justin, and Pauline have all been looking forward to your arrival. I'll take you to YWAM, and I hope we will soon be working together again."

They walked together to his car. Cary was filled with joy, trusting him, his pastoral friends, and the Lord.

CHAPTER TWENTY-SIX

"Hi, Jill. I'm so glad to talk to you. How are you doing?"

"I'm working, day by day. Calling around and speaking about the LRA situation. I'm heading to an early lunch now, and you're probably dealing with work. What's up with you?"

"Well, I wanted to call you earlier today but got side-tracked by jobs on the phone. However, I came back to Soroti a few days after you left, and I'm stuck in a YWAM sleeping area that is pretty scary and dangerous for me. Nice ladies, but the windows are cracked, the mosquitoes found the holes in the net and I got dive-bombed. I woke myself up by whacking myself in the head several times. And the dogs howl, and it is hot. I have to keep my sheet over my head to avoid the 'flying attacks'. More people have come in to this area, some from horrible situations, so I can't complain. But I know you'd understand."

"I do, Cary. I don't have mosquitoes here. As you would say, 'Yippee'!"

"Well, you made me laugh now. I needed that! I've been so sweaty today I decided to not go to the office until tomorrow. The pastors have been working elsewhere, so I don't feel too guilty that I didn't head downtown. And..." Suddenly, Cary heard someone banging on the door. "Hold on, Jill, I've got to grab the door."

Cary opened it and was surprised to see Joseph. "What's up?"

"Cary, I really need you to go to see the lady we've mentioned to you before who only has weeks to live. I want to take you there now. It's been pressing on me all day, but I haven't seen you downtown, so I decided to find you here."

"Joseph, give me about five minutes. I'm talking with Jill and I need to change my clothes, and I'll meet you in the front."

"Thanks, Cary. I'll wait. Oh, and say hello to Jill for me."

"I will." Cary rushed to the phone. "Well, Jill, Joseph popped in and I need to go meet that lady we've been told about who has a serious cirrhosis. In our world, it's often because of too much alcohol, but that's not the case here. I've never met her and he wants to take me there now. He says 'Hi' to you and I have to say 'Goodbye' to you. I'll let you know what happens when I'm back."

"I'll pray for you two. Be in touch when you can. Bye."

"Goodbye, Jill. Bless you."

Cary changed her dress, put a cap on her head to hide her unkempt hair, grabbed her purse and camera, and ran out. Joseph was talking to Diana, who was in charge of this area of the YWAM compound.

Diana nodded at Cary as she walked up to them. "This is a very important way to touch her heart, and to take care of any of the young ones she has on that outside veranda. Thank you both."

Cary stepped out of the front and climbed in his car. "Where are we going?"

"To the PAG."

"In all these weeks I haven't learned what 'PAG' means. I know it's a church, but that's all."

"Pentecostal Assembly of God. There are thousands in our nation. I am sure you've seen some of them before."

"Of course. I should have understood that a long time ago. And probably did a few years ago when James and I lived here." She grinned. "I can be forgetful at times."

"We'll be there in a few minutes. I want you to meet her and pray for her, and then we will go out and get her a few things." He looked at Cary seriously. "With the hundreds of needy people in the PAG area as IDPs, they will crowd around you in hopes you can give them something. We'll only focus on her. Her death and needs are very important."

"OK. I'll try to do the best I can. If you want me to do something, turn someway, you tap me on the shoulder and I'll do whatever you say. Oh, and are there any issues besides her health that I should know?"

"Yes. I forgot to tell you. What happened to her has been quite common these past months. Her husband and two of her sons were murdered while fighting the LRA group that was invading their village. She's older than the young lady you saw in the hospital whose little babies were murdered. Her sons were in their upper teens."

When he drove in, he parked near the building where she was on the veranda. Cary was shocked. She was sitting there with six kids. At least some of their needs were very obvious. Broken mattresses and dirty sheets were dotted around. None of their clothes were very good, although some were not too bad. Cary didn't see any food there. And the woman's stomach was *huge*, even though her body was very thin.

Young children ran towards Joseph and crowded around him when he got out of the car. Obviously, he was well-liked. He smiled and gently told them that he and Cary were here for this lady and her family. They stepped back a bit but did not leave. They waited, watching Joseph and Cary.

Cary got out and reached for the lady's hand, and she gave Cary a grateful look. Joseph greeted her and talked with her. He did not bother to translate for Cary.

Joseph asked Cary for her camera, and then told her to sit on the edge of the veranda with the woman and pray for her and he would take proof of this with a photo.

Cary prayed. "Dear Father, I know you know all of us everywhere. All I can ask this time is that you will continue to touch her heart and her body, heal her here or take her to heaven. That's what all of us face. All we can do is trust you. Also, Lord, please touch the hearts of these kids, because they look so angry, so frustrated and hurt. With their dad and two brothers murdered and their mother seriously ill, please pour out your love and touch them. Thank you, Lord. Bless you."

When she finished, Joseph talked to the lady momentarily and then tapped Cary's shoulder and pointed at the car. Cary nodded and bowed to the lady, then she hurried over to the car and jumped in.

"What are we doing next? The mattresses and clothes all looked bad and I didn't see any food. I know the PAG has had some people come in and help, but when there are hundreds of people staying there, it'd be hard to provide for everyone."

"We will buy blankets, and we'll go to one of the churches close to downtown and we can choose vegetables, flours, and cooking oil. Let's stop at a blanket shop first."

"Sounds good. How much do we need to pay for blankets?"

"Sorry, Cary. I forgot to indicate that the purchase must be from *you*. I have very little money, and with those hundreds of people in my church yard I cannot keep up with the needs. Including feeding my wife and girls."

Cary smiled. "That's OK. I have quite a bit still. You and the other pastors are more important than what I'd grab for me. So pull in where you need to."

They walked through a shop not far from her office. Cary chose six thick blankets, large enough to spread around.

The shop cashier checked through them and said, "Madam, this is twelve thousand." Cary smiled. That was equivalent to about twenty-five dollars, which was a very reasonable price. She paid the twelve thousand gratefully.

"Cary, now we will go to Church of Uganda. That is large and has different flours. You'll meet some of the workers. I've known them for a long time."

When they walked in, Cary was pleasantly surprised to see at least a dozen workers sorting through the piles of fruits and vegetables, other foodstuffs, and charcoal. Several families stood in line, some people holding babies. It was a real treat to witness. The pastors' wives were in charge of this. Cary and Joseph left with a large amount of the flour. On the way back to the PAG church, they stopped and quickly bought some oil and a few of the other things necessary for cooking.

"When we're going in, Cary, I will quickly put it all around her, and you take a quick photo from inside the car, because we will need to leave quickly. Otherwise, many of the other people will want to grab us to get things for them. We'll drop it off and we'll leave."

"OK. I'll pay attention. Please tell her that she is on my heart."

"I will. I believe you have entered her heart, too. As we often say, when we can't get together on the earth, we can get together in heaven."

He pulled in and quickly unloaded, and the family seemed very pleased with the gifts.

When they left, Cary turned to Joseph. "That little boy looked about two years old, much younger than the others. He seemed out of place next to the older children. Do you know anything about him?"

"Yes, I do. Her brother's wife is dead, her brother left town, and he left this little boy to his sister, expecting that she will care for him. She certainly does."

"I don't know enough names here in Soroti, unless I have a chance to write them down. Do you?"

"Actually, no. Thousands of people have arrived in town these past few months, and there are too many to remember their names, which is not the way I like to minister. In my own church I do know more names. It's a very hard time we're going through. I hardly have enough time to be with my wife and children. I'm looking forward to when the Lord will let these people go home."

"I'm glad. Thank you."

"I'll drop you off at YWAM and you might have time to rest. You've been very helpful, and I greatly appreciate it. Thank you."

"I'm very happy about sharing today. When I get in, I'll be calling Jill nearly immediately to unload all this information to her. Then I'll be calling my pastor at home, Pastor Max. He'll share this with my kids, my friends, and the church. They have the Lord in their hearts, too."

Joseph stepped out of the car, opened her door, and when she stepped out he laid his hands on her. "Father, in the name of Jesus, I lift Cary to you, and I thank you for bringing her to us and for the time she took today to help that special lady and her family. Please fill her with a blessed evening and a restful night. We trust you, moment-by-moment. Amen."

Cary smiled and thanked him. Even though it wasn't what one did outside of families, she gave him a quick hug. She walked into the building and headed for her room, looking forward to visiting with Jill and resting.

She was smiling again as she walked into her room and said, "Thank you, Lord, for your love and your encouragement, and that I could help others today. It was a blessing. I started my day filled with frustration and tiredness and anger and now I'm filled with joy. Again, thank you. Love you, my Father. Bless you. Amen!"

CHAPTER TWENTY-SEVEN

Cary opened the door to the office, planning to head out soon after to interview more of the kids in the Rescued Children's Camp. She was surprised to see Joseph, Jacob, George, Job, and John there, discussing how they could help the people in their church yards. They nodded at her, and she went to the back of the room and sorted through some clothes.

"I need to go over and interview the kids again. Do you need me to do anything now? If not, I will look for David to take me on his bike."

"No, Cary," said Jacob. "I need to go to my house, so I will take you there. You can find you way back, I'm sure. Call me if there's no other way."

"OK. Thanks." Cary turned and suddenly looked at George. "George, what's wrong? You don't look at all well."

"I have malaria, madam."

"Have you taken medication?"

"I can't afford any, so I'll wait for the Lord to heal me. He's done it for many of us before. My dear friends and family and church members will be praying for me. Many of us with malaria must just suffer through it. Have you ever had it?"

"Yes, James and I had it at the same time in April 1995. Even with the medications, it took us quite a while to become healthy. After the worst was over, James had severe headaches that lasted weeks into the summer, and I had stomach pain and tiredness that lasted a few weeks longer than his did. I am taking a preventative now, but it might only lessen the effects." She paused. "Unless you say 'no', I'm going to get you medicine."

George and the others looked at her. Cary saw them nod at him. She ran out of the office and down the street to the pharmacist. The pharmacist chose some pills to treat the malaria and put them in a bag. The cost was quite low. She grabbed the pills and ran back up and gave them to George. He thanked her profusely.

"Jacob, can you take me now? I want to spend time with the kids. Their stories always touch my heart as well as others' hearts."

"I can leave in about ten minutes. I hope you will have a wonderful time there, and I know they will be blessed through you."

Cary smiled and went to the back of the room again to sort through the clothes. It was an easy but important part of her job. She wanted them to be ready in case Pauline came to pick up clothes for kids who were in need.

A few minutes later, George came to her. "Thank you, dear sister. I appreciate how the Lord used you to help heal the malaria. I'm sure my wife will be pleased." He smiled and said, "I need to go home now, take the pill, and rest for a day. I should rest more, but there is so much to do. I hope to see you when I come back to the office." Cary smiled and touched his hand.

When she turned, Jacob nodded and said, "I'm ready to go, if you are."

When they reached the children's camp, the Teso Arrow guards men recognized her, nodded, and let her walk into the yard. Then Susan came out and waved, walking over to her quickly.

"Miss Cary, I would like to spend time with you, of course, but there's a large group of missionaries here, and I'm showing them everything in all the tents and rooms, the cooking area, and housing for the sick ones. You are welcome to visit, but you may not want to tour with them—you already know much more than they do—and you can see I can't translate."

"Well, OK. I'll stay a few minutes anyway, and see some of the kids if I can. I don't want to try to find a *boda* now."

Susan smiled, nodded, and walked away. Cary wandered slowly to the other side of the area and noticed about half a dozen girls playing volleyball. Cary smiled at them. The girls smiled back and one of them tossed the ball at her. Cary grabbed it, and tossed it back. For about fifteen minutes the ball was tossed up and over and around, and she ran into the middle. They surrounded her and started tossing the ball to each other, and Cary would jump up and grab the ball and toss it up high so someone would get it.

When she was done, she walked over and handed it to a girl that seemed to be leading things. Cary waved at the girls and walked to the boys and the guards who were watching and laughing. Cary said, "This was so much fun! I haven't done this for many, many years, even with my grandchildren. I loved it and I'm so happy that you enjoyed it, too."

"How do you feel, Madam?" asked one of the guards, because her face, hair, and dress were quite sweaty.

Cary swiped at her face and her hair. "Oh, I'm way too hot because of this playing, but I'll be fine, once I drink some water. What a day!"

The people laughed, and some thanked her for coming. She smiled and waved and walked out.

Cary decided to walk on the lanes that went around the Soroti Rock, around to where the town had most of its shops and homes. Cary would like to have climbed the rock, but she knew she wasn't up to it. She walked for about a mile, and suddenly she heard a car honk. It was Joseph.

"Cary, I was looking for you, and I'm so glad I saw you here. You look very hot, and you probably haven't had enough water to drink. Climb in and have this water. I'll take you either to the office or to YWAM."

She grinned as she climbed in. "Perfect timing. Thanks for the water, too; I need it desperately. Let's go to YWAM because I need to take a shower. I was going to try to find David and have him *boda* me there."

"How did things go with the kids? Did you interview more of them?"

"No, there was nobody to translate. Instead I played ball with the girls, and all the kids and guards laughed. That was worth getting hot and sweaty. Before when I've walked around or interviewed the kids, they've only seen me looking very serious, sometimes teary. Now they've seen me laughing and jumping. It was a treat."

"Well, I'll drop you off at the complex and you can go in. Day after tomorrow—Sunday—I will pick you up and take you to my church. I have wanted you to attend, and since you are leaving in about a week, you must come this Sunday. The people have heard of you, some have seen you, and they will be thrilled to have you there."

"Thank you so much! It will be a blessed morning. I can hardly wait. Tomorrow, I'll spend time here, meet more of the workers, and I'll go through my clothes and determine what I can leave behind. I usually try to leave as much behind as I can. That's why I bring so many extra clothes and shoes." They arrived at the complex, and she climbed out and waved goodbye.

CHAPTER TWENTY-EIGHT

Cary put on the new Ugandan dress she had purchased a few weeks earlier in Kampala. She wanted to look nice for Joseph's Baptist Church service. She had just finished dressing when her phone rang.

"Aunt Cary, I'm here now. Come as quickly as you can."

"I'll grab my Bible and my purse and I'll be there in a minute."

It didn't take long for them to reach the church. Cary had often passed it and had taken pictures of Joseph and some IDPs who were staying on that property. It was nice to see inside the church this time.

Pauline saw her. "Oh, Cary. I'm so happy you came. Will you sit with me?"

"Yes, I will. I know that Joseph is busy pastoring and taking care of his family and the IDPs. So, you're stuck with me, sister." Cary gave her a quick hug.

Cary was amazed at the number of people in that church. Pauline told her it was about five hundred adults. Many of them were from town and more than half of them were IDPs. Some wore nice clothes, while others had torn shirts and nearly ruined dresses or pants. But they treated each other joyfully and with great respect.

When Cary saw the children she grabbed Pauline's hand. Some of the kids wore shiny shoes and fancy hats and stood next to the other kids who were barely dressed in rags. Even the kids were filled with joyfulness and smiled and grinned and tapped each other and laughed. Cary had never seen that kind attitude in the States.

The service began with worship and all the people sang in their own languages. They lifted their arms and rejoiced. Joseph was the youth pastor but was in charge that day, and Cary was excited to hear his words and his heart for the people.

"Aunt Cary, please come to me so the people can hear something special."

Cary was very surprised. She stepped up as he continued. "People, this is a spiritual warfare woman who has entered our lives. We have shared very closely about what has happened and how the Lord can come to our area and pour out his strength for us. She shared with Pastor Job one day, and she doesn't know that he talked to our pastor group about it. I didn't tell her ahead of time that she is today's main preacher. I will explain this again, and in more detail, at church tomorrow evening. Now, Madam, please say what you will." He smiled at her and touched her arm as he went to sit down.

"Thank you. As Pastor Joseph said, I did not anticipate this, but I'll share as clearly as I can.

"Pastor Job and I have talked about the fact that the Teso and the Karamojong named each other with curses attached. The fighting and unrest between the two tribes have continued for about four hundred years. It began when a large group of people rushed from the Ethiopian area. They ran together for days and days, maybe months. Then one large group of them determined that they couldn't go further, as they were too tired and had families that couldn't climb the mountains. They were in the northeast portion of what has now become Uganda. The other group, mostly young men, told the others that those who stayed behind did so because they were not brave enough to go on. They called them a very bad name and headed over the mountains and the hills. The ones who stayed behind were furious then at these young men, but they couldn't go. Years and years later, the Karamojong who had stayed behind became very dangerous, and they often still are today. I was told a few years ago that when they had come to the Lord they were shocked and surprised that they had to stop killing people. The Teso group became less strong than the other overall, but the slander and fighting and murders have continued. Now, Pastor Job intends to connect with Christians there and pray about the horrific demonic warfare and attempt to turn this around. This is significant. I realize you can't change tribal names, but God can show you how to reverse this curse, possibly by repentance between Christians of both tribes in some significant location. You can at least start to think in that direction and see where and how God leads you. I have shared much of my spiritual ministry with Pastor Job and many in our nation and other nations. It is important to know the historical events that permit satanic powers to take over. Many of you here are dealing with Joseph Kony's demonic service. As I recall, he took over from his aunt who had begun this. Many are abducted, abused, and seriously hurt. Some have turned to the Lord and broken out, and they are doing all they can to help others. I'm a very grateful woman, because so often in other nations of the world, people do not step forward as strongly as my Ugandan dear ones have. Thank you for letting me share, and I hope it will help you understand more of your own background so things can change."

Cary smiled and started to sit back down, but she stopped. "I'm sorry. I didn't tell you the verses the Lord laid on me for my ministry a long time ago. I need to grab my Bible." She went to the seat and picked it up. "OK. Here are the verses. First he gave me Isaiah 42:16. It says, 'I will lead the blind by ways they have not known, along unfamiliar paths I will guide them; I will turn the darkness into light before them and make the rough places smooth.'" She looked around and many people were nodding.

"Here's the other one. Amos 2:9. It might not sound right, but the Lord laid it on me years ago, and he has not changed it. I'll explain it after I read it. 'Yet I destroyed the Amorite before them, whose height was like the height of the cedars, and he was strong as the oaks; yet I destroyed his fruit from above, and his roots from beneath.' Is it a little confusing for you?"

Many of them nodded. "I have many friends who are used by the Lord as the *fruit* people to deal with serious sin and to work hard at turning it around. In many nations, for instance, abortion is accepted. Many of my friends go to where abortions are done to tell people it is not acceptable and it should not be done. They are very strong and very brave. Then, the Lord uses me—and others—to search for the *roots*. The purpose is to look for the history or foundation, the sin or events that gave Satan entry into a house, an area, or nation. Once a root is known, then it can be dealt with—through prayer, or renunciation, or blessing. In your case, maybe something in your tribal background is causing serious problems. Some of you will be 'fruit' people while dealing with what is happening now, and some of you will be 'roots' people so the background connection can be broken. Figure out how the Lord wants to use you. Not all of you may be involved. God uses all of his people in different ways, in different situations. However, if he happens to call you into a certain situation, he will show you what to do and where to go and how to bring his peace, joy, glory, love. Now I will sit down. Thank you, Joseph, for giving me this sharing time."

Joseph smiled at Cary, and as she returned to her seat, the people began to clap loudly. Pauline was so happy to have heard her; she intercepted Cary before she could sit down and gave her a hug. They sat down and Cary was filled with gratefulness at being used by the Lord. She had no idea that she would share this topic with anyone other than Pastor Job!

CHAPTER TWENTY-NINE

After Joseph preached for a while, he asked pastors whose villages had had to flee from Kony to stand up. More than forty men stood. During the following worship time, people lay hands on the pastors and prayed for them.

Towards the end of the service, a man stood and began speaking. Cary didn't understand his tribal language, but she could see that people were overwhelmed both with sadness and with joy. Pauline looked shocked, wide-eyed. Many people, including Joseph, immediately prayed for him.

At the end of the service Joseph brought the man over to Pauline and Cary. He spoke openly to Pauline, who translated for Cary.

"My name is Moses and I am thirty-seven years old. When the rebels in our village grabbed me and my brother, they made us carry the heavy artillery weapons and said if we dropped a gun or damaged any of it, they would kill us. We carried these things all around the northern area of Uganda for hundreds of miles, in and out of the forests, up and down the hills, across the streams. We never broke anything.

"Our rebel captain was particularly evil. He decided to kill me. He beat me with a panga[1]. I collapsed, and the captain was very happy because he thought I was dead. But suddenly, I stood up. I had painful cuts on my body, but I was able to carry the weapons.

"A few weeks later, the captain commanded the *other* rebels to beat me until I died. The captain wanted to show the others how much power he had. They obeyed him and beat me with their rifles and other weapons. I fell, and they later told me I really appeared dead. Then, a few minutes later, I stood up straight. I told them that it was the Lord who had healed me and given me strength.

"A few days later, the captain issued the same command. This time, the others slashed me with pangas. They cut me all over; I was bleeding heavily from my head and other parts of my body. My feet were damaged and one of my toes was cut off. I collapsed again. They were certain I was finished.

"Very soon after, I stood up. I had again been healed enough to move around. I still had the cuts, but the Lord gave me strength to stand straight.

"The captain was furious. He again told the others to kill me. They said, 'No.' He said, 'I am your *captain*. You do what I tell you to do.' Again they said, 'No!' He said, 'Then I will kill him.' They said, 'He has come back to life three times. If you kill *him*, we will kill *you*.' No one touched me again."

He showed Pauline and Cary his head and his scars from the panga blades. He also showed them the scars on his feet, and the toe missing. He smiled at them. He said he was happy in the Lord to be alive.

Shortly after his last beating, he managed to escape.

When the Ugandan Army found him, he was taken prisoner. Since he was older, they were certain he was with the LRA. He was found near his home village, and some of the villagers recognized him as someone from their area, so he was set free.

Now he was staying in Soroti at a local camp, because he did not want to be recaptured. Even though he knew the Lord had brought him back to life, he didn't want to face that danger again. He also was happy to be reunited with his family here, and did not want to be separated from them again.

After he was done with his story, Cary had Pauline ask if he knew anything about his brother.

He shook his head. He looked very concerned for a few seconds. Then he smiled. "I can trust God for him. When I was captured, my wife was very near to having our fourth child. I did not know if I would ever see my family again, and now we are together here. If God could do that, he can take care of my brother".

Cary turned to Pauline. "His body is so abused—all those cuts on his head and his feet! Is there anything we can do for him?"

"We can pray for him. As it was for Ipullet's brother, it is true for Moses—the hospitals are so overloaded that he will not receive any care. There are others who need it more. The Lord truly kept him alive. He would rather spend time with his wife and children than go to the hospital. He trusts the Lord, and that's all that counts with him. I'm so sorry for him, but he's very content."

"If I could ever return to Soroti, I would love to find him and see how things come out for him. He smiles so much, and he is so happy to be with us."

Cary took a number of photos of Moses' feet and his head. When they finished sitting together, Moses smiled and thanked Cary and Pauline for listening to him.

Pauline and Cary smiled at him, stood up and headed for the main door. Joseph was talking with many of the church people and the IDP people on their property.

"I'll take you home in a few minutes," Joseph said to Cary. "I planned to take you to our house so you could have dinner with my wife and daughters, but I have to go out of Soroti to one of the large IDP areas to check on some of the people that others are looking for. I'm so sorry, because you are truly a special person. The people found your information about the tribal history helpful. Some knew it, but many did not. This will open more hearts to the spiritual background. Instead of hating the Karamojong, they can lift them up to the Lord. I would like to be in that portion with Job. He's a wonderful pastor. I appreciate him. Oh, and why did you tell him all of that?"

Cary thought back to her time with Job. "He came into the office to get some money, and he asked a question about history because of the consistent warfare that had persisted for many generations, and I shared what I knew with him. He realized more of it suddenly, and he told me some. As he left he said he was glad he came by himself to get money because we could talk without interruption. It was only for an hour, but we covered a lot. I also told him about other areas of Uganda that I had studied when I anticipated being a missionary years ago. So he's not the only one who has heard of their local spiritual history. It's been a blessing to share."

"I'll take you to YWAM very soon."

Cary and Pauline sat together and smiled at all those who walked past thanking them.

1A large cutting blade with a handle, like a machete; used for cutting plants.

CHAPTER THIRTY

"Pastor Max," Cary said into the phone, "Today is my last day to go to the Rescued Children's Camp. Many of them have gone back to their families at other IDP places now. Also, the LRA has begun to retreat to their northwest area, so some people are heading home, hoping to repair their property, plant some vegetables, get some chickens or goats or sheep, and fix their roofs. Hundreds of the kids are gone. They feel it will be safe for a few months, if the army can keep the LRA away. I'll head out and let you know what it's like. If nothing else, I'll be writing about what it is like here."

"It's good to hear from you. I know you have a lot on your plate and I look forward to seeing you and hearing much more. How long?"

"I'm supposed to leave here in three days, four at the most. Then I'll be in Jinja for an extra night, I hope, then to Kampala for a day or so, and then the airport. If it all works out, I'll be home in about a week. I can hardly wait. I love it here, and I miss being with Sam and Adhe and hope I'll have a day with them before I hit the plane, but I also miss Jill in England, and all of you at home. I'm really struggling. I always say though, that when I get to heaven my family and friends from all over the world will be together and worshiping our Father. That's what counts."

"Yes, that's so true. I look forward to seeing you. Get in touch when you can. Have a great day with the kids."

"Thanks. I feel much more comfortable now, because you've been a blessing as usual. Please send my love to people."

"I sure will. Bless you. Goodbye."

"Goodbye."

She hung up, joyful and smiling. She walked outside and waved at the people walking through the YWAM area.

David was waiting there with the bike. She had her backpack in case she needed to write down events, to be emailed home later.

David drove skillfully down the side lanes, past the IDP camps. Everyone smiled and waved to her now that they recognized her and knew what she was doing.

When they reached the place, David said he would come in and stay with the Arrow army men and would wait for her. She greatly appreciated that. She thanked him and she decided she would give him a little extra money later.

"Is Susan here?" she asked the guards.

"No, Madam. She had to go to an IDP camp for now. You are free to walk around if you like."

Cary went towards the main portion where she often interviewed the children. It was hot outside, but she could sit on the shaded veranda. She found a chair and sat down.

A little while later a teenage girl walked past; she looked shell-shocked and ashy. Her eyes were vague and distant, very sad, and she walked slowly and focused only on the ground. Cary wanted to get up and talk to her, but felt that it was not something she could do. So, she prayed for her and watched her.

Suddenly, two boys came up to her.

"Madam, can we talk to you? We would like to do that!"

"Yes, you can. I always look forward to hearing from any of you. You can tell me your stories."

The boys sat on the floor and introduced themselves.

Cary smiled at the first one. "Simon, how old are you?"

"I'm thirteen. And I'll tell you much of my story and you will laugh, Madam. I'm sure you will."

"Then you talk. I'm looking forward to hearing it. Although you have been with the LRA, you certainly smile a lot."

"In the middle of June, I was digging in my parents' garden when the rebels came and grabbed me. It was very hard to be there and to see so much. So many of the ones with me were beaten, some killed, others forced to carry heavy loads, and we weren't given food very often. Many were very hungry and had to serve food to the rebels, yet were not allowed to eat any of it. That was very hard."

"How many were in your group? I've heard so many different numbers."

"Our group had about one hundred rebels and about one hundred and fifty of us. We moved from one part of our northern country to another, partly because there were so many people and they needed to be sure to have enough to eat and drink and stay alive."

"How long were you with them, and how did you get away?"

"Well, I'll tell you." And he began laughing, "After six months me and another boy from another part of our country were told to go stand down on the road to watch out for the army and then run back and let them know. The rebels were hiding in the bush area. They knew the army was coming. Then we were by the road for a while and none of the rebels showed up to check on us. And the army did not show. I smiled at the other boy and said 'Let's leave.' We did. I never saw him again because he ran in a different direction, to another part of our country. I've been here for a few weeks, and workers are looking for my parents at an IDP camp so they will know I'm alive and I'm here. I'm very happy."

Cary smiled. "I've never heard anything this wonderful. I hope you truly understand that the Lord protected and kept you."

Simon smiled. "Yes. I'm happy. My parents will be worshiping and thanking God."

For a few minutes the three of them talked more. Then Cary glanced up and saw the teenage girl she had noticed earlier. The boys looked at Cary and said, "Have you seen her?" Cary nodded.

Simon said, "I'll tell you, but it is very sad. She was in one of the rebel groups with her best friend. The rebels grabbed her friend and cut her throat, and they told this girl that if she cried, they'd do the same thing to her. I don't know how she got away, but somehow was able to get here. She is still very, very sad. I hope her family can be found, but she hasn't said much about where she is from. We are trying to help her, but the girls and our leadership, especially Madam Susan, are still having a hard time. Madam, you are a pray-er, too, so I know you will do that."

"What is her name? I will pray and have my family and friends pray, also. And boys, it was a true God-gift for me to hear the story from you, and not hear it from her. I'm sad from hearing what you have told me, but if I had heard it from her, I would have been crying too much. Now I can pray."

"We don't know her name. Many of us don't use our names, anyhow. She does not talk to any of us very often. We only know about the murder of her best friend and the threatening. I smile much of the time and laugh much, as you've seen, but I don't laugh or smile about what happened to her."

They finished talking, and the boys left. She went over to where David was waiting and asked him to translate for the guards.

"Thank you so much for protecting these people. I'm glad I came here and have seen many who are safe now. It is difficult to hear the stories and I've often cried. I also know that many of them and you are serving our Lord. This is my last time to be here. I'm going to be flying home from Entebbe to the States in just a few days. You are heavily on my heart, though, and I appreciate you very much."

They nodded and thanked her heartily for her work.

"David, now you can take me downtown so I can check into the office. I will be there only about a half-hour, and then I hope you will be able to take me to YWAM. Do you think it will work out?"

"Yes, Madam. I will take you anyplace, anytime. When you leave I will feel very sad. You have been a wonderful helper."

"Thank you, David. Let's grab the bike. I won't be seeing the Soroti Rock very often, now."

She climbed on the back confidently. She chuckled to herself, remembering how she had been so afraid the first time. Now it was fun and she felt safe—most of the time.

She waved at the guards and the kids as the bike drove off. They waved back, showing their appreciation for Cary being part of their lives. Cary loved them and knew she would miss them when she left Soroti.

JOANNE NORTON

CHAPTER THIRTY-ONE

Cary heard a knock on the door in their YWAM room. It was Anne. Cary realized they hadn't spent much time together, even after Allen and Anne had come back from Jinja.

"Cary, Allen and I would like to have you go to dinner with us. It's at the Taj Mahal café. I know you've been there before. We're paying. You don't have to bring a purse or any money of any kind."

"Well, how sweet. I would never have thought of something like that. I'd love to be with you, especially since I'll be leaving soon. What time?"

"If it's convenient, we could leave in about half an hour. But if you need to rest after your day at the Rescued Children area, we can go later."

"Half an hour is fine."

Anne started to turn away, and then turned back. "I forgot to tell you that we will be riding bikes. We have three. We'll ride across the park area, and the paths are usually pretty good. But dress in something you can ride in, and wear your tennis shoes. Come over in about a half hour. We look forward to time with you." She gave a big smile.

Cary wore a long skirt, a hat, and tennis shoes. She hadn't ridden a bike for years, and here she had only ridden as a passenger on a *boda*.

She walked to their side of the complex where Allen was taking the bikes out of the garage. He wheeled one over to her. "We're sad that we haven't had more time with you, so this will be nice."

Anne came out, and the three of them got on the bikes. There weren't many people in the park, but the few there waved at them.

Cary wanted to wave but wasn't sure she could keep control of the bike. So she nodded her head and smiled.

They stopped at the back of the café and tied the bikes together.

At the Taj Mahal Cary witnessed a common occurrence: the waiter gave them menus, heard their orders and then said, "Sir and Madams, I'm sorry, we do not have that today." Eventually they gave up and asked what was available—and they took it. Chicken, baked potatoes, mixed vegetables, and lots of chai tea.

Cary smiled at Allen and Anne. "It's fun to be together. That's all that counts."

"Cary, I heard that many pastors and others have gone to one of the largest IDP camps northeast of here on a big truck, filled with clothes, food, and lots of water bottles. Knowing you a bit, I'm surprised you stayed here."

"I wanted to go at first, because Job, Justin, Jacob and Pauline asked me to go. I nodded, but behind them I could see Joseph shaking his head 'No' very strongly. I went out of the office to ask him about it. He said that if I went, and if the rebels attacked the truck, it would be especially bad for me, as a white person. Joseph said that sending me home to my kids and my pastor in a coffin would be very sad. He felt strongly that the trip would be dangerous for me, and I obeyed him."

"Did anything come up that would have been serious?"

"Well, Joseph called me shortly after they returned. There were about fourteen thousand people at the IDP—very large. There were two water hand pumps, but only one was working. They desperately needed water and the IDPs were horribly upset, but they couldn't go anywhere else. It wasn't dangerous, but Joseph said I would have been heartbroken."

"I'm glad you didn't go. I'm also very happy that the pastors returned."

"I hope I can see a few of them before I leave. They've been such a blessing. You have been, too!" Cary smiled at them.

An hour later they'd finished. Cary thanked them for buying her dinner and thanked them again for loaning their room to she and Jill.

Cary suddenly laughed and explained to Allen that he taught her something no one else had since she'd been in Uganda as a missionary or visitor. "Remember when you taught about using a hole-in-the-ground latrine—with no toilet? Even at your not-young age, when I first got to YWAM, you showed me how to squat with my feet very *flat* on the ground, so I could do what I needed without falling in the dirt. You're a strong guy."

They laughed together. "Well, I've been in a number of nations in Africa for about twenty years, so I had to learn how to do it. I didn't want to touch the side sections to keep my balance, because the spiders or roaches or snakes could be there."

"I've had that happen, too. I did touch the sides a few times, once in the Murchison Falls park, for instance, and a big spider was right there while I was trying to keep balance. That was very scary. My friend Kathryn worked in Kenya as a nurse with YWAM, and when she was in a latrine there, a python was hanging from the top. She was able to get out before it hopped down." She grinned. "I'm looking forward to going home where it's safer. But *you* are funnier."

They left the café, and Anne and Cary crossed the street on their bikes. Allen stayed behind to pay and ended up talking to one of the waiters. They knew he'd follow them soon.

Suddenly Anne's tire went flat, and she nearly crashed. Cary stopped to help, but she soon realized they'd picked the wrong side of the street. It was lined with trees in which sat hundreds of pelicans, as they were not far from the lake, and they were pooping. It hit their hats, clothes, and hands, and it smelled horrible. Allen came and grabbed Anne's bike and took it across the street. He told Cary to head for home.

As Cary rode off and glanced around, she noticed a group of men who stood by, laughing. Their mistake had amused a whole audience.

Cary had to ride the bike through the park area again, this time alone. It was dark, and she was a bit frightened. She did it, but she sometimes had a hard time staying away from the edge of the lane and the holes. She could also smell the foul odor from her hat and shoulders. She reached the YWAM yard a few minutes later and was glad to find there weren't many people hanging out.

Cary ran to her room, grabbed a towel, soap, and shampoo, and ran over to the other side of the compound where she could take a shower. Even if she had to bend down, since it wasn't high enough to be over her head, she would do it. The clothes and tennis shoes were dirty and stinky. She had to scrub everything. She had to let the water go down, wipe the shower floor again, and then wash and rinse again until the smell was gone.

Finally clean, she headed back to her room. She put the wet clothes in a plastic bag so she could hang them in a side portion of the room. Looking out the window, she saw Allen and Anne and she ran out. The three of them talked for a few minutes. Allen and Anne said they would be moving to England in a couple months and never coming back through YWAM either, because now they were in their sixties and the work was getting too hard. Cary reminded them that she was heading home soon and might not be able to ever come back.

Cary was back in her room checking the clothes she had hung up to dry when someone knocked on the door. It was one of the youth.

"Madam, pastors have come and they are in the teaching room. Come, please."

She hurried over.

Pastors Job, Justin, and George sat in the room. Job said, "Sister Cary, we want to pray for you, because we know you are leaving soon. Let us all stand together and hold hands and I will begin." They did quickly. Job said, "Thank you, Father, that you sent Cary here for the spiritual warfare information, so I would learn and teach my church. Again, thank you, Lord."

Job nodded, and Justin began. "I appreciate my spiritual sister, Lord, for helping Pastor Job to deal with the people that have been calling me a foolish man and trying to stop me from pastoring. Now I'm safe. Also, Lord, thank you for using her to help the family next to me when that little girl was burned. The family is happy now, because she looks very good. Please bless dear sister for us, Lord. Thank you."

"Thank you for using her, Lord, to purchase malaria pills for me. I'm doing so much better already. My church is so happy. If I ever feel so ill again, malaria or anything else, I will try to reach to a doctor who will help me. Thank you, Lord, because now I've changed my attitude."

After the prayer time, they all laid hands on her shoulder and prayed for safety and health. As they left, Cary touched each one and said, "I look forward to seeing you in heaven. I would love to see you here again, of course, but since I doubt I'll be back, heaven is the only opportunity we have. The three of you, and Joseph, Jacob, and Pauline and other encouraging people have been a huge blessing. Again, thank you so much."

They waved and smiled as they headed to Job's car.

Cary stood on the porch for a few minutes. She lifted her arms to the Lord and said, "Thank you so much, Father. You told me to come. Sometimes it was wonderful, and sometimes I was surrounded by sorrow and fear. But you have helped, encouraged, and protected me and many others. I'm grateful and I appreciate you. I love you so much, my dear Father."

She returned to her room and sank gratefully into sleep, dreaming of home.

CHAPTER THIRTY-TWO

Cary was startled from sleep when her phone rang. She rolled over and answered it. "Hello?"

It was Joseph. "Cary, I know you planned to leave tomorrow, but I am driving to Jinja to talk with another pastor today, so I can take you that far. You don't have to go by bus. If you want to go with me, could you be ready to leave in an hour?"

"Oh, that's wonderful! I certainly don't *want* to be on the bus. An hour may be too tight, though; could we make it an hour and a half? I'll jump up now and do all I can as quickly as possible."

"OK. I'll wait that extra bit of time. I can certainly spend an extra half-hour with my dear wife and little girls. I'll probably be back here late tonight, but seeing them any time is a good thing. I'll hang up so you can start."

"I'll work hard and fast. See you. Thank you so much."

Cary jumped out of bed. She grabbed her backpack and filled it with books, her journals, extra pens, and several socks, make-up, combs and hairbrush. As she crammed the rest of her things into the other large duffle bag, some people walked into her room. One of them said that Joseph had called them.

"Madam, I am sorry you are leaving so soon, and I know you had much for us, but we want to give you some of the clothes and shoes so when you are in Jinja or Kampala, you can give them to others."

"Thank you. Yes, I will take them to others. The important thing is that the poor get what they need."

They gave Cary the shirts and shoes, and she thanked them. It would add to her load, but she wanted to get them to Kampala.

Cary hopped into the bathing area and cleaned up quickly, then dressed in her jeans and a very long shirt. She knew she could wear them in Jinja and Kampala and she could relax more easily. Before leaving, she ran to the other side to say goodbye to Anne and Allen. She then found the main local YWAM leader, Diana, and thanked her for her consistent help. Then she called Joseph. "I'm ready."

Ten minutes later, Joseph pulled up, and Allen carried her heavy duffle to the car. Joseph got out and put her duffle and backpack into the trunk, then directed her to sit in the front. As she slid in she glanced in the back seat and suddenly laughed.

"Jacob! You're here! I'm so happy to see you. I haven't seen you these last few days to say goodbye. What a blessing!"

Jacob smiled. "Joseph invited me to go to Jinja with him, and I agreed. He then said, 'I'll be asking Aunt Cary to go with us. If she will do it, we will be together with no one else interrupting our time, as usually happens.' That made me even happier to ride with him."

Many people had come to see them off. When Joseph started the car, they heard dozens of the YWAM-ers saying "Goodbye" in a variety of languages.

"Thank you so much, Joseph. To be with you and Jacob and *not* be on a bus, I'm overwhelmed with joy. You are quite a sweet and caring son to me."

As they were leaving town, Cary turned around and waved at the Soroti Rock. "Goodbye, you big and beautiful rock. I'll miss you forever." Joseph and Jacob smiled.

They talked about everything on the way to Jinja, and they reached there shortly before lunchtime.

"Where do you want to be dropped off, Cary?" Joseph asked.

"My friends Fred and Josephine have a shop on the main street which sells artistic pieces for tourists. If we drive down that street slowly, I'll see the shop. We met and became friends when James and I attended their church in 1991, and we remained in touch over the years. She and Fred have also become YWAM members and use their shop as an opportunity to plant the seed of God in tourists and Ugandans and other Africans."

Soon she saw it on the left side of the street. "Pull over. I'll run in." Joseph pulled over to the side of the street, and Cary ran to the shop and pushed the door, but it didn't open. "Oh, dear. Where are they?"

She decided to pound on the door, if nothing else. The door opened after a few knocks, and Josephine screamed joyfully, grabbing her. "Oh, dear sister, it's been too long since I've seen you. I'd hoped to see you before you left, since I had heard you were in the Soroti area." She hugged Cary tightly.

"Did you see Anne and Allen when they were here a month ago?"

"Yes. They are leaders. So you know them, too?"

"I was able to stay in their bedroom, which was cleaner and a bit larger than the other YWAM room in Soroti. My friend, Jill, and I had some time until we had to leave for Kampala. I said goodbye to Anne and Allen this morning. When you see them, tell them we're friends with you. I hope you'll see them before they head to England."

She glanced back at the car. "And these are my pastor friends from Soroti who brought me down here." She waved at them to come out and they walked up quickly. "Joseph and Jacob, these are wonderful YWAM people."

They talked for a while, and suddenly Cary asked, "Where's Fred?"

"He's at the Nile right now. He's counseling a couple who are having marriage issues. I think he'll be there for another few hours, but we can go there. I'll take some food with us so we can sit there, and we can walk and eat till he's free. What time do you need to go to Kampala? Can you stay here overnight?"

"I'm only here for about three hours. I need to get to Kampala and be at the hotel before dark. But I sure want to spend some time with you, honey." She turned to Joseph. "Can you drop us off? It's only a few blocks away, but that will save us some time."

"Yes, Cary. Let's go now. We'll go to the church for our meeting as soon as we drop you off."

They got in the car and headed to the Nile. When there, Jacob and Joseph hugged Cary and told her they loved her and looked forward to seeing her again. They thanked Josephine and waved a last goodbye.

Cary and Josephine carried the bags to the tourism building and put them inside to be protected by the police. Then they went down to the Nile near to where Fred was meeting with the couple. As they arrived they saw him shaking hands with the husband and wife, their meeting finished. Fred then saw Cary and Josephine, and he ran to them, arms wide.

"Cary, my dear sister, it is a blessing to see you. Of course, my dear wife, it's always a blessing to see you, too." They went down to the river and walked past the tourist boats. After learning about her schedule, Fred said, "Hey, sister, do you want to take a ride? It's only an hour and we can eat on the boat, and then take you to the taxi area. I'd love to take you to Kampala, but I don't have a car. The taxi's the best you can do."

"I've never been on a boat here—I would love that. I've only gone walking around as far as I can and sitting on the rocks." She smiled at Josephine. "Do you remember when James and I were with you in another part of the Nile, when we sat on the big rocks at the edge of the river? It was so much fun!"

"Oh, yes. That *was* a lot of fun, and you and James were on the *boda-bodas* and I had been on a bus and waited for you there. I can't forget that; we laughed so much."

"I have pictures of it, too. You took one of James and me while sitting on the rock, and James took one of you and me. I'll never forget that day."

Fred said, "Then let's get on the boat now. I've arranged it with the men. It doesn't cost much, and the river isn't flowing too quickly, so we won't bounce around." He took their hands and walked them to the boat and they sat. It left soon after.

Cary was amazed. She asked Fred about a building they passed, and he told her it was a prison, and that the prisoners worked at the farms in the area.

"Oh, the birds!" Cary grabbed her camera and took pictures of the egrets on the trees that were in the midst of the river, right at the point where the lake became the river.

Fred said, "When you look to the side over here," and he pointed there, "there's the sign that says to stay away from the crocodiles, because they are near the lawn area and they will attack anyone."

As they looked, they saw a crocodile right near there that was cut in half. "Oh, yuck!" Cary said. "I don't like them, but I don't like to see things cut in pieces like that."

It was a perfect day to be on the Nile and on Lake Vic. Cary loved it. The three of them did a lot of talking in a short time because she had to leave soon. The boat returned on time, and after they paid for the tour and added a tip, they got her duffle and backpack and walked to the edge of the Nile park. There was a taxi right there, and the steward confirmed it was going to Kampala. When six people were in the taxi, the driver would leave, and then stop in town and other locations on the highway until they were filled with fifteen. Four people were already in there, so she told the driver

JOANNE NORTON

she'd like to join. Josephine and Fred gave her a big hug. Fred loaded her bags onto the back and she climbed in. The driver left five minutes later, and the three of them blew kisses and waved goodbye.

The taxi ride went well, with several people being picked up along the way. They looked at Cary curiously, not used to seeing a white woman riding.

Suddenly her phone rang. "Oh, Sam, I've missed you so much, and I'm leaving earlier. Can we get together in a day or so, before I leave?"

"Mom, we were home for a week, and I thought I could pick you up any time, and if you could, we'd love to have you at our house before you leave. But I got a call two days ago and had to go to my mother's again. I will try to be at the hotel to take you to the airport. You call me any time, and I'll get to your place as quickly as possible, with Adhe, Stella, and Rebecca. I would cry if you left before we could see you. I'll really try hard, Mom."

Cary said, "Honey, I'll let you know when the timing is in place. I miss you and your family very, very much. Since I'm in a taxi right now, I need to hang up because the phone doesn't stay open very long. I'm very happy and very blessed that you called. Please share my love around."

"I will, dear Mom. Love you so much. All I can say now is goodbye."

"Goodbye, son. Thank you for calling."

Before she reached Kampala, Cary began to feel ill. She was very weak and tired. She was shocked at how quickly it happened, when it hadn't hit her this strongly in Soroti or Jinja. A few times in Soroti she'd been very tired and felt a bit weak, but this was the worst she had ever felt.

As the taxi pulled into the Kampala taxi area, Cary knew the only thing she could truly do was pray. "Dear Lord, please help me. I can't help myself very well. You are all I have, so please, please, please help me. Amen."

CHAPTER THIRTY-THREE

Cary looked and felt very tired when entering the Kampala taxi area. It was huge, with hundreds and hundreds of taxis. She looked around for the "private-hire" taxis—small cars that would take one to a specific place.

When Cary climbed out, she put the backpack on her back, which she did not like to do because that made it an easier target for thieves. This time she had no choice. She also carried the heavy duffle bag. It was wearing her out, but in a block or so she'd be able to put them in a car.

A few minutes later, as Cary was walking towards the side, a young, and not strong-looking, teenage boy stepped towards her and asked if she needed a car. Cary nodded.

He insisted on carrying her duffle bag, hefting it easily. He started moving quickly away. Cary, tired as she was, moved as fast as possible, concerned that when he went past the shops on the edge of the taxi park, he would hand the duffle over to somebody stronger to run away with it. She hurried and kept him in view.

Suddenly Cary realized God had given her an angel. She didn't know all the details yet, but she felt God's peace in her heart despite her fear.

When they reached the street, he said he would find a special hire and asked Cary how much she wanted to spend. Remembering how much it had cost those weeks before to go from the hotel to the taxi area, she said, "It will be seven thousand."

He said, "No. Unless it's not very far, you can pay only five thousand."

Cary was shocked at his honesty. If he had hired a car, he could have arranged with the driver for seven thousand and taken the extra two thousand for himself.

After they left the parking area and were standing on the side of the street, he asked, "Do you know why I am helping you? I have a sister in Norway and she said I should help people and not expect anything back. My sister said that Pastor Benny was on TV and that we should bless our elders and then God would bless us."

Tears poured down her cheeks. In her exhaustion and illness she truly felt God's gentle and very timely care.

"What is your name?"

"My name is Joseph."

Cary smiled. "There are many Josephs here in Uganda."

"At many of our churches, we know who Joseph was in the Bible and we want to be like he was."

"How old are you?"

"I'm fifteen, but I am smaller and weaker than a lot of the others. I do what I can and I listen to the Lord."

Joseph went to find a car and driver and arranged for the money. He also got in the car and went to the hotel with her.

Cary needed to break her Ugandan twenty thousand to give them their five thousand, so she asked them to wait. "I gave my smaller bills to the previous taxi. When I left Soroti I didn't realize I only had larger bills left. As soon as I check in, I'll arrange with a secretary to give me change."

The driver and his friend nodded and they stood outside by the entry door. Joseph came in with her and stood off to the side of the desk.

At the reception desk, she bent down to get her passport out of her backpack. Suddenly, she started to faint. She tried to hold on to the side of the desk, but she couldn't stand up. The desk receptionist called one of the hotel men instantly and the man rushed over and took her to a chair in the lounge. Joseph followed and sat near her.

In a few minutes, the dizziness faded. She looked at Joseph and asked why he had come, even though she appreciated him.

Joseph said, "I wanted to escort you, because God put us together. I also wanted to come because I have never been in a hotel and I wanted to see what it was like."

When Cary was finally able to get the money changed, she paid the driver five thousand. Then Cary gave Joseph two thousand. Joseph was very upset. "I shouldn't have this much, Madam. Five hundred is good, but this is too much."

"Joseph, you did much for me, and the Lord used you, so the Lord told me what to give to you. He is blessing you for helping me. I will give it, and the Lord will bless both of us for doing what he calls us to do. Thank you."

"Thank you, Madam. My mother and sister will thank you, too." He smiled and walked out.

JOANNE NORTON

CHAPTER THIRTY-FOUR

Shortly after Cary was shown to her room upstairs, a housekeeper knocked on her door and came in. Cary was in bed.

"Madam, I was told to come up here now and prepare you to go to one of our doctors. It is not a hospital, but there is a doctor and a nurse, and it's a good clinic. You will be driven there by one of our men. So, please dress as soon as you can, and come downstairs, and we will send you. We are very concerned about your health."

"Thank you so much. I'm not certain what is wrong, but I do want a doctor. I'll be down in about fifteen minutes."

When Cary walked down the stairs, one of the men stepped right up to her and said, "I will take you now. And I will wait outside during the treatment, take you to purchase medicines, if needed, and then bring you here. Let us go."

He held her arm and took her to the car and drove a couple miles away, and took her in. The nurse immediately took Cary to a room, and had her lie on a bed. It was very small and uncomfortable. The light was too bright, and Cary asked for it to be turned off, but she was told that if one light was turned off, then all the lights would be go off. The walls were not all the way to the ceiling, but only about seven feet tall. Cary lay down and covered her face with a towel so the light wouldn't hurt her.

The nurse came in and put a needle in her arm and drew out blood. It was very painful, and although she didn't scream, she shuddered. The nurse said it could be tested very quickly and she could rest. About a half-hour later, the doctor came in.

"Mrs. Nolan, you have malaria. Are you surprised?"

"No, Doctor. I have just come from Soroti, and there were many mosquitoes there. I had malaria in 1995, and I recognize it now. It took me four months to recover then. So what do? I want to head home soon, and I don't want to be sick on the plane."

"On the way to your hotel, stop for the pills. This is a newer drug, and it should work better for you than the old medications. If you leave in three days, you might be able to make it home reasonably well. You will be tired, but other than that, you should be fine. We'll give you the best we can."

"Thank you. I will rest. And my hotel desk leader will contact the airport and check the flight schedule. Hopefully I can rest for three days."

"I hope you do well. Thank you for coming."

The driver stepped in and nodded at Cary. They walked out, he put her in the car, and they drove downtown and stopped at a pharmacist. She went in and, in about five minutes, she received the malaria pills. They returned to the hotel.

Cary thanked the driver and gave him a tip. When she went upstairs and settled down, she called her daughter, Sue. Cary knew that Sue might be taxiing kids around, but she knew Sue would want to hear this, so she could share the information with Pastor Max and everyone else.

"Sue, do you have time to talk for a few minutes? If you can't, I'll call Pastor Max or Mike. Up to you."

"Mom, take as much time as you want. That's what counts. I sure want to know when you're coming home. We miss you!"

"I'll probably be leaving here in three days, depending on the airline's schedule. I'll try to keep you and others up to date. But the main thing I have to tell you is that I have malaria. I've been very tired, with a bad headache and stomachache. Nothing as serious as it could be, but I ain't running around town."

"What do you need to do, Mom? Malaria is serious."

"Well, I've got pills to take, and I'll rest. All I can do. However, this will make you grin. I just saw a doctor, a nurse, and a pharmacist, and I bought malaria pills. The total cost was equivalent to twenty-eight dollars. The hotel is not cheap, about a hundred dollars every day, but at home this medical bill would have been hundreds and hundreds, too. I came out pretty well."

"Again, Mom, what do you need to do?"

"I'll just rest, and look out the window for birds. I'll try to eat, but I have to be careful. I'll drink what I can. I need to make sure I'm near the bathroom."

"OK, Mom. But let me know."

"I think Sam and Adhe will be coming here tomorrow or the next day for sure. They want to see me, of course, and I want to see them and give them hugs. I don't know if anyone else will show up, so I'll do the best I can to get ready for flying home." She paused and then said, "Oh, and I still need to arrange to give away the clothes and shoes that were given to me by the YWAM people. I want them out of my duffle, because I sure don't want to drag that extra weight around. I'll try to send it out with Sam and Adhe."

"Good idea. I'm happy to know you will be home soon. Love you so much."

"And I truly love you and the others, too, so please spread my news around."

They both said, "Goodbye. Love you," and hung up. Cary took a shower, and then read Revelation for a while. The pills had started to work, and the nausea had lessened. She went to sleep.

JOANNE NORTON

CHAPTER THIRTY-FIVE

Cary went down to the restaurant and bought a biscuit, bacon, and chai tea. She sat on the balcony outside her window and spoke to the birds.

"Hello. It's good to see you, stork. At least, that's what I've been *told* you are, even though you often dig in the dirt."

Cary smiled. Even dirty birds caught her attention. Then her hotel phone rang. She walked to the bedside and picked it up. "Hello."

"Mom, it's good to know you are there."

"It's a huge blessing to hear from you, Sam. I've been here one long day. I came mid-afternoon before that and became quite sick. I have malaria. Spent yesterday mostly sleeping. Feel a bit better today. Are you coming?"

"We will be there in a couple hours. I would love to take you around town, but if you're too tired, staying there will be fine. Stella and Rebecca will be happy to be with you. Maybe we'll go to the back side of the hotel and sit by the palm trees and enjoy ourselves."

"I'm happy. You come and we'll talk and talk, and talk some more. Or at least I will." She laughed and Sam chuckled. "See you soon, honey."

"Yes, Mom. As soon as we can."

While she was waiting, Cary went down to the desk area and asked, "Do you have a suitcase or a duffle bag or anything similar that has been left behind? I could buy one from you."

"Yes, we do. Last week someone left a bag in a room. We tried to contact him, but we haven't heard back. Since he's in India now, we won't keep it. You would not need to pay. We did not buy it, so you don't have to, either."

"Thank you so much. I am going to unload the clothes and shoes I was given in Soroti. I will put them in this and give it to my Ugandan son who is coming, and he and his wife can give them to a number of families who are in need. That will be a blessing."

"Thank you. I'm happy to give the suitcase to you." She walked to a closet, brought it out, and gave it to Cary.

Back in her room, she went through her duffle and was able to fit everything in the suitcase except for a few pairs of shoes. She set the shoes aside; Sam or Adhe could take them in a bag. The duffle was nearly empty except for a few of her own clothes that she'd kept, and it was easy to lift.

Sam and Adhe and the girls came in an hour later. "Oh, what a blessing to see you again. I didn't want to leave without spending a few hours with you." They all hugged.

"Adhe, I have clothes and shoes I was given in Soroti, and I was hoping you could pass them to the families you know. I hope all of them will appreciate what other Ugandans have given. Maybe hearts will turn to other areas of the nation and to the other tribal groups. That's very important to me, to say the least."

"Mum, I'm so happy. Thank you. I'm already thinking of some of the families that need these and will be grateful. I'll tell them that the gift is from Soroti."

Sam came in from the balcony and whispered, "Take a look. Rebecca never been in a hotel or anything similar, of course, and to step on the balcony she put her toes out and tapped to make sure it wouldn't fall. She was pretty scared—even though there's a chair out there and she can see people on the other balconies. She's a brave girl at our place, with cobras or pythons or big spiders, but places like this make her react more fearfully."

Cary went towards the door and reached out to Rebecca. "Dear, are you doing OK now? Do you see the birds? They look happy, so I hope you are happy, too." Cary reached around her and hugged her. Rebecca nodded slowly, and walked very carefully, looking where she would step. They went inside together.

"Where is Stella? I saw her, I think, but don't see her now."

"Mom, she's never been in a room like this, and she's trying to crawl under the bed. It's bigger than anything she's ever seen." He reached down and pulled her out. "Hug your grandma, Stella. She loves you very much, you know."

Stella was put into Cary's arms, and Cary kissed her forehead, her cheeks, and her chin.

Sam asked, "When do you leave, Mom?"

"Tomorrow morning, about 11:00. The doctor said I should wait three days, but if I didn't take this flight, I would have to wait four more days. I need to be there by ten at the very latest. It can take nearly an hour to get there from here when the roads are so full. I can take a taxi from this hotel."

"No, Mom. *We* will take you. I already thought of taking the girls with me to stay at the Baptist church because they have a room for visitors. I know I can stay there, especially since my cousin Andrew is still the pastor. Adhe will stay with you and that will be a blessing for her."

Cary smiled. "It will be a blessing for me, too. We've spent a bit of time together, but this alone time will be truly special."

"I will leave in about an hour and take them to the church, and we will come back at about eight in the morning. You can have a whole evening together and I think that will be a blessing for both of you. I gave her money for dinner, so you do not need to pay for it at all."

"Thank you so much. Oh, and what's going on with your mother? We've gotten so sidetracked that I've forgotten to ask."

"Well, after we drop you at the airport, we'll head north to her village. She's weak and she's sick often. I've taken her to a doctor, and the doctor has done what he can. We'll go back and show her our love. We *might* have to take her home with us, and she would stay in the room you were in. To have another loving mother in that place so soon would be nice." Sam smiled and gave her a hug. "We're sad to see you go, but because of the special time we've had, we're also filled with joy. I love you, Mom. So much!"

"Me, too, son. It's truly been a God-gift to see you, and now your family, too. I'm going home, but I can never forget any of you. You'll always be on my heart. James loved you very much, too, and he'd certainly love to see you and Adhe. We loved the wedding when we came over for that. So we often say we look forward to seeing our family and friends in heaven when we get there." They both smiled.

Adhe was with the girls on the balcony but soon came inside. "I thought we would go down in the back under the palm trees, but the girls love being inside here. Seeing the birds straight ahead in the trees has made them smile and laugh. When they get to church, they can play with friends there. You and I can relax and rest and rejoice together, Mum."

Cary went down to the car as Sam and the girls were leaving and gave hugs to them all. "See you in the morning."

Sam set them in and kissed Adhe goodbye, then smiled with love at *this* mom.

They waved happily when he drove off.

Cary and Adhe sat outside by the palms with sodas, pomegranates, pineapples, and bananas. They stayed there until well after dark, and shared for hours about the way the Lord broke into their lives, when both of them were in very difficult family situations.

They talked easily about their families and serving their Heavenly Father, even with the difference in their ages and experiences as God's daughters. The moon was full, lighting up the night.

After they went to their room, Cary took a shower, packed everything she had, and kept out what she'd wear in the morning. Since it would be cold when the plane landed in Europe, she put her jeans, thick socks, sweatshirt and jacket where they'd be easily accessible.

They prayed together, shared some verses that were special to them, and went to bed. Cary prayed as she was going to sleep, thanking God for his kindness and protection. Her heart was filled with hallelujahs.

CHAPTER THIRTY-SIX

"Mom, we're here. Are you ready, or should I come up to help?"

"We're ready. Since you already took the heavy suitcase, Adhe and I will have no trouble coming down. Give me a few minutes. I also want to let the hotel desk people know how much I appreciate them for sending me to the doctor and giving me the suitcase. They have been very kind."

"Come when you can. I'll just keep the girls here by the car and they will have fun looking at the birds."

"See you in a few."

Cary and Adhe finished looking through the bathroom for soaps and shampoos and anything they might be missing. Also, since Stella had gone under the bed, Adhe looked to see if anything had been left under there. Both places were clean.

At the desk, Cary talked with the clerk. "Thank you and your wonderful workers here, for blessing me. I will pray for you that the Lord will increase your hotel tourists and increase your wonderful workers. If I ever did come back to Kampala, I would stay here again. I will tell others about you, too, and tell them to stay here when they come to Uganda."

"Thank you, Madam. We appreciate your kindness. We would love to see you again."

They left, and Sam and the girls ran to them, gave them hugs and held their hands while walking to the car.

It took about an hour for Sam to drive Entebbe, park the car, and walk in together. Even though the plane was leaving an hour late, Cary had to say goodbye to her Ugandan family. They stayed across the room, could talk on the phone, and could wave and blow kisses.

When Cary went into the plane, they climbed up onto the top of the building with many others. All the people watched the plane as it was filling.

Cary found her seat, arranged her things, and made sure her pills were at hand. It would take eight hours to get to London. Even though it was daytime, Cary hoped to sleep well enough that she could make it through the rest of the waiting time. However, she didn't sleep immediately.

Cary sat next to a doctor from England who had been in Uganda for two years. He was a very nice man and allowed her to unload about the malaria and how difficult her work in Soroti had been, how she'd seen and heard so many wounded and heartbroken people.

"I assume you have malaria medication. Is it working?"

"Yes. I'm still tired, but it's much better even after just two days. When I get home tomorrow I can rest."

"Do you feel emotionally drained after all you saw and heard?"

"Yes. I hardly can ever get it out of my mind. I am constantly going over the memories of what they shared with me at the camps. I call that a God-job, and I know he is protecting and keeping me. But the tiredness from that is significant. Maybe if I was younger it wouldn't be so hard, but it certainly is now."

"You can check with your doctor when you reach home, but I think you might have post-traumatic stress. That certainly can cause many physical symptoms. Also, tiredness, frustration, anger, and other symptoms can take weeks or months to show up once you are back in familiar territory."

"I thought of that before when I was in Soroti, but since the malaria I had forgotten it. I'll have to call home before I leave

England to let them know about it. They'll have to put up with me in the coming weeks." She smiled at him.

"It helps when family understands these situations. Since you've been with wonderful people in Uganda, which it sounds like is true, and you will be with wonderful people when you are home, the PTSD may not affect you long." He smiled at her. "Now, as we are five hours from England, I'll swap seats with you so you will be next to the window. I will give you a pillow, and you can take a nap. Rest. You need it."

They changed seats, he got her a pillow and she used it against the window. She thought she might relax but not be able to sleep. However, she fell asleep immediately.

When the plane landed, she woke up. She thanked him and he smiled. Free of the plane, she walked through the airport where she would get on a plane to New York, and then to St. Louis. She had a three-hour layover and decided to call Jill.

"Jill, I was so excited to be here and hoped that you could come, but the time is short and I'm too tired to walk far, so I don't think it's going to work. I'm so sad."

"Cary, I couldn't be there, anyhow. I'm in my hometown, Worcester, and am going over to church. I wanted to stay in London with my sons so I could get to the airport to see you. I hoped to take you out of there and go downtown and have some girl time, but it hasn't worked out."

"James and I went through London a few times when flying in and out of Uganda, and sometimes we had twelve or more hours between the flights, so we did a lot in London. I'd love to be there again, and specifically with you this time. Maybe eventually I can come over to stay with you for a few weeks. Let's see how it happens."

"I'd like that. Is there more to tell me about Soroti? You have kept sending information my way, but I didn't know if it was everything."

"I'll write you a long letter when I'm home. I can tell you some snippets about the pastors. I love them so much. After you'd left, they spent more time with me to protect me and keep me involved with them and their people. They also took me to see people who were struggling. Have you ever heard of the medical condition called PTSD?"

"Yes, I know that. Why do you ask?"

"I sat next to an English doctor on the plane, and he said this could be a possible issue. I was feeling pretty awful in Soroti right before I left, but when I reached Kampala, I found that I had malaria. Medicine is helping me with that, but it feels like there is more wrong. It may be PTSD. When I get home, I'll have to spend a fair amount of time resting, instead of running around to see people. Hope they'll be patient with my fatigue."

"I'm sure they will, from the way you've talked about them. They love you."

"Well, I love you very much, Jill. I'm so grateful that we were able to work and share together. And thanks for putting up with me. That was a real treat!"

"God put us together. It was fun. Oh, I'm so sorry, but someone is knocking on my door and I have to head out to church."

"Well, Jill, give yourself a hug from me, and I'll hug me from you. OK?"

"Yes! Thank you, sister."

As they hung up, both hollering "Goodbye" and both laughing, Cary smiled for a few more minutes. Then, estimating the approximate time she'd be in St. Louis, she called Mike.

"Hey, dear son, I can hardly wait to see you and Matthew. What a treat to be with you when I get off the plane this time."

"When will you get here, Mom?"

"Maybe twelve to fourteen hours. Don't bet on that—I can give you a more accurate time when I get to New York. I'll call you then."

"I can hardly wait to see you, Mom. Are you going to call anyone else?"

"I'm going to call Pastor Max now, so he'll know I'm done. He's been very supportive."

"OK, Mom. I'll look forward to hearing from you. Love you."

"Love you, too. Bye for now, kid." She hung up and picked up her backpack, heading to the plane. "Thank you, Lord."

EPILOGUE

Cary found her seat on the plane and settled in. She then called Pastor Max.

"Pastor, it's Cary. I'm leaving in a few minutes and will be home in about ten hours, depending how long it takes to get through New York. Mike will pick me up in St. Louis, and I expect to be there before midnight."

"I will come to see you about noon tomorrow. I want to give you plenty of time to sleep, to rest, and to enjoy your kids and grandkids. Then I'll pop in."

"Look forward to seeing you, and I'll tell you so much about Soroti that I hadn't included on the phone or email. I look forward to being home."

"Bless you, Cary, and I'll be praying for you again all day and all night."

"Praying for you, too."

"Thank you. As I've indicated, I can hardly wait to see you. Goodbye for now, though."

"Yes. Goodbye. The plane is beginning to turn around and head out."

As Cary headed home, she felt a strange mixture of solemnness and joy. Even though her time in Soroti had brought her face to face with struggle and heartache, she had met wonderful people and had been able to help many. Spending time with Sam and Adhe and the girls had been a treat. Meeting Jill was a God-gift. Her joy outweighed her sadness.

While resting on the plane, she silently worshiped and thanked her heavenly father. "God, you are forever the treat of this world. I can hardly wait to see you, either here or in heaven. You are all that counts." She turned to look out the window. "And, Father, I'm looking at the ocean, the sky with the clouds, and I'm filled with joy. I see *you* in the clouds. Thank you for using me, for healing me, for loving me."

She leaned back on the seat, worshiped her Father, and went to sleep.

THE END

DEDICATION AND EXPLANATION

The first, of course, is my dear personal Lord and Savior. Not much else could ever count.

I want to acknowledge my long-time dear family and friends (including those I know from Facebook and blogging) who have supported my writings. Too many to name, but they are a blessing.

The book is partly fictional, but there are many real people.

1) Samuel and Adhela Serunkuma, and their daughter Stella are the most important. Samuel has been our Ugandan son for 20 years. When he married Adhela in September 1999, she became our daughter.

2) Jill Pogmore from England has worked at New Hope Uganda for about 15 years. She was a hard worker with and for me in Soroti. She has become a wonderful sister for Dave and I.

3) The pastors and others in Soroti were very important and helpful. I still have connections to one in particular. His real name is Joseph Opio-Edulu and was referred to as "Jacob" in the book. Many of the other pastors listed are real. In fact, I recently received an email from Joseph that indicated that George (the pastor for whom I had bought malaria medication), misses me and loves me still.

4) The couple in Jinja, Fred and Josephine, whom Dave and I have known since 1991, have been wonderful friends. They are still involved in YWAM, and have been helping many in other African nations.

5) The "angel", Joseph, who protected me in Kampala at the taxi area, truly was a blessing. Before leaving, we sent money to his mother for his schooling.

6) I did have malaria, and it did hit me at the hotel, and the staff members there were as wonderful as I wrote them to be.

My husband, Dave, referred to as "James", is a dear, special man. After I had been serving for ten weeks, he came for two weeks, before we went home. After that, it took several months to recover from the stress. The combination of malaria and fatigue on top of the heartache and suffering the children shared was extremely difficult.

I thank the Lord for telling me to go. He enabled me to do the job He placed on my heart. I'm grateful He allowed me to see my former Ugandan friends and for giving me many new dear friends there. I thank Him also for protecting me and letting me worship and serve Him then, and now, and forever.

JOANNE NORTON